I0760363

ASSASSINATION IN THE GLADE

A VIKING WITCH MYSTERY

CATE MARTIN

Cover design by Shezaad Sudar.

Rune art by BettyStrange at Dreamstime.com.

Ratatoskr Press logo by Aidan Vincent Kise.

ISBN 978-1-958606-63-6

Formatted with Vellum

CHAPTER ONE

JULY HAD COME into Villmark as a vicious wave of stifling heat, hot and still and so humid it was like my clothes never once felt completely dry, even as I was wearing them.

Then, two days after the Fourth of July, all that still heat had exploded in the mother of all thunderstorms. It raged for a night, then a day, and into the next night. I hadn't seen the like of it since moving to the north shore of Lake Superior the September before. The fall had had its gales, and the winter had been as cold and snow-buried as I had expected.

But this? Thunder and lightning for thirty-six hours? It had felt like the gods were angry with us.

All I had been able to say to keep myself calm was at least we were too far north for tornados. Although I wasn't even sure that was true. It might have just been a comforting lie.

But that storm passed, as all storms do. And I woke up to a perfect day. Everything felt fresh and clean, warm but not too hot, and no hint of humidity. There were tree branches fallen all over Villmark, but cleaning all that up was almost a pleasant chore when it was such a lovely day to be outside.

My little courtyard hadn't seen much damage. After sweeping a few leaves off my stone tiles and replacing a broken potted plant, I had no more work to do.

So, on total impulse, I sent my black cat Mjolner to invite my friend Loke and his sister Esja to visit.

My cat Mjolner, in addition to having six toes on each of his front paws, can also walk through walls and cross vast distances faster than a human can run. Not that I've seen him do these things. I've just seen him show up where he shouldn't be, just when he was needed. And he had fetched help for me just in the knick of time on more occasions than I really wanted to count.

I had no idea how many times my life would end up in jeopardy when I had come north after graduating from art school. I had thought I'd just stay with my grandmother until I was on my feet, making enough of a living as a book illustrator to afford my own place.

But then I'd taken up the mantle of being my grandmother's apprentice, perhaps one day to fill her shoes as the volva—the wise-woman—for all of Villmark.

Although, frankly, that shouldn't involve finding my life in danger as much as it did either. I shiver to say so, but the truth is I'd gotten used to it.

So it felt a little weird sending Mjolner not to fetch help before some adversary got the better of me, but to invite two friends over for brunch and partaking of the view out of my huge south-facing windows.

But Mjolner didn't seem to mind. He just looked up at me with his intelligent green eyes, and then he darted away in that way cats do, going from complete stillness to ballistic rocket in the blink of an eye.

I had no worries that my invitation wouldn't be understood. I tried not to feel bitter about it, but the truth was Mjolner and Loke understood each other better than Mjolner and I did. It was almost like, when I wasn't there, the cat could speak words that Loke could hear.

Maybe someday I'd be able to hear him too. I was learning more and more every day about rune magic and being a volva, like my grandmother and great-grandmother before her. Speaking to a cat was small potatoes compared to some of the things my grandmother could do. But I was still very much a beginner.

While I waited for Mjolner to return, I ran to the market for fresh-baked cinnamon rolls and an assortment of fruit. I had crispbread and pickled herring already in my kitchen, and enough coffee to keep all the mugs full even if all five of the Thors showed up.

More properly called the Valkissons, the brothers we all called the Thors patrolled the wilds around Villmark. The middle of the five, Thorbjorn, had been my closest childhood friend. I had forgotten him just like I'd forgotten all of Villmark for all of my teen years, but once I had returned, the two of us had picked up that friendship just where we'd left off. We saw each other as often as we could.

Which was never as often as we'd like. Especially lately, with more and more dangers emerging from the wilds inside the magical world around Villmark, patrolling was too important to take more than the smallest, most necessary of breaks from.

It was rare to see more than one or two Valkissons at a time, given their duties, and rarer still to see all five at once, but I liked to be prepared. They kept the village safe from all manner of threats, from things as mundane as wolves or bears to things as out-of-the-norm as trolls or the Wild Hunt.

The least I could do, given all that, was to make sure they never had to wait in my kitchen while I went out for more coffee.

Mjolner hadn't returned when I got back from the market, but it was a far shorter walk to the market a block from my house than Loke and Esja's home far to the south of Villmark. So I wasn't worried. I just put my purchases away in the kitchen, then went out into my living room and started moving my easel as well as my spare easel both to a place conveniently close to those windows.

The view really was breathtaking. Villmark was built on the top of a tall hill. The expanse of Lake Superior was just visible to the east, behind rows of tall trees. To the west were ever-taller hills covered in even more trees. The spiky tops of several kinds of pine jutted out from a dense sea of various clumps of green from the birch, ash, maple and poplars. The fall colors were famous in this part of the world, but July wasn't too shabby either.

But the real gem of my view was the south view the windows were built to frame. The lower two-thirds of Villmark were arrayed before me, each row of rooftops just a shade lower than the one closer to me. Then the village ended, giving way to wildflower-studded pastures. A few cows and sheep grazed there.

If I squinted just right, I could make out the spot where Loke and Esja's house nestled between a pair of hills. The trees around it were in full leaf now. It was easier to see in winter. But I thought Esja would appreciate the different perspective on her home all the same.

I had just finished adjusting my easels when there was a knock on the door. I passed Mjolner in the hallway. His job done, he was heading to his bed in the sunniest corner of the living room to take a well-deserved nap.

I threw open the door to see Loke, dressed as always head to toe in black, with his sister Esja close beside him in a lightweight gown of snowy white. She was clutching what I knew even without the copious colorful stains was her art bag filled with her watercolors and pads of paper.

She looked completely comfortable, her thin, pale blonde hair pulled up in a braid crown with only a few loose tendrils to cling to her sweating brow.

How Loke wasn't absolutely dying in all that heavy, black cloth was a mystery. But I couldn't see any sign of sweat on him.

"Thank you so much for inviting me out, Ingrid!" Esja said as she pushed past her brother to pull me into a quick hug. Then she was gone, as if she already knew there was an easel in the living room with her name on it. I hadn't told Mjolner about it. But of course Mjolner *would* just know.

"Hey, Ingy," Loke said, using the nickname I only just tolerated from him. But I didn't call him out on it today. No, I was frowning at him for an entirely different reason.

"You look tired," I said.

"It's nothing," he said, too dismissively for my tastes.

"You look worse than your sister," I hissed at him.

"Hush! Don't let her hear that," he said, as if I hadn't already lowered my voice.

"What's going on?" I asked.

"Nothing but the usual," he said. Then indicated for me to move inside so we could shut the door.

I didn't like that nonanswer. I mean, there *was* always something going on with him. He had power that neither he, I, nor my grandmother completely understood. And he had very little control over it. So that was, one could argue, *usual*.

But since he never wanted to talk about it, dismissing it as if he didn't want to rehash it again was a bit much. We'd never properly hashed it in the first place.

"Oh, Ingrid! It's just gorgeous out there today!" Esja called from the living room. "Look at those clouds, so puffy like giant sheep. Nothing like the haze we've had for days and days. But you have to show me where my house is. I don't think I know the way well enough to pick it out."

"*That's* why we're here," Loke said to me with a sly grin. He was clearly pleased to have our conversation interrupted by his sister's enthusiasm before it even got started.

But he wasn't wrong.

The month before, in the days before the big wedding between one of my closest friends, Kara, and the youngest of the Thors, Loke and I had found ourselves trapped outside of Villmark, unable to return. The magical barrier that protected all of Villmark from the wider world's knowledge had become impassable, and we had been stuck in the modern Minnesotan fishing town of Runde.

For me, it had been mostly a matter of feeling like I had been to blame for that somehow. I was so new at the magic I was meant to be good at.

But for Loke, it had meant days of not knowing if his sister was all right. His sister, who was sick on the best of days, and deadly sick on the worst of days. He had been in agony.

And Esja had been... just fine. She had come into town to stay with some of my friends until Loke could come back. For someone who was rarely well enough to have visitors, let alone go visiting, she had found it a rare treat. But one marred by not knowing where her brother was.

Since then, I'd made Loke promise to bring her back into Villmark more often on her good days. And I knew she had been to visit Kara's sister Nilda a few times. Even more surprisingly, she had called on Sigvin twice. Sigvin, the poor young woman who had the worst unrequited crush on Loke.

I was curious for more details on how *that* visit had gone, but I doubted Loke would be up for sharing.

Anyway, today Esja was visiting me.

"I assume there's food in your kitchen?" Loke said as he walked away from me, towards that open doorway. "Why don't you join my sister in the living room? I'll get the food all plated up and bring it out after the two of you are both so thoroughly lost in your world of art you don't even know I'm there."

"Thank you!" I called after him. He just waved a hand back over his shoulder.

I went into the living room to find Esja already clamping a sheet of watercolor paper to the drawing board on my second-best easel. She smiled up at me, but only for a flash of a second. Then she was digging through her supply bag, finding things she wanted and arranging them around the easel.

"Do you see the road that runs out of town?" I asked her as I pointed it out. "The stones glow like silver in the moonlight, but it stands out nicely from the grass even in the sunlight."

She paused in what she was doing to squint out the window. "Yes," she said at last.

"Okay, follow that line until it reaches two hills that run in long ridges sort of parallel to us," I said, tracing what I meant with a fingertip. "Your house is there, snug between those long, low hills."

"Oh, yes," she said, a happy flush rising up on her cheeks. "I recognize the elm there. I can see it from my bedroom window. How lovely to see it from here."

Considering how badly their Victorian home had fallen into disrepair since their parents had died in a fire inside that very house, this view where only a peek of roof tiles was visible was indeed the loveliest view.

Esja had settled on her chair and was already sketching in what she wanted to paint in the softest of pencil lines. I sat down at my own easel, but watercolors had never been very much my thing.

For magic, I preferred the messy, open-to-interpretation art I could create with charcoals.

But I wasn't doing magic art today. I was just passing the time with a friend. So I, too, started sketching in the tree-covered hills to the west. Trees were so fussy to draw with pen and ink, but I really couldn't help myself.

Ink was my favorite. And I really loved trees. I was already considering the techniques I'd use to make the birches distinct from the elms and the maples. There were at least six distinct shades of green out there. And I was going to convey it all with black ink on white paper.

It was some time later when I sat back, distracted by the growling in my stomach. The sun had shifted visibly across the sky. Considering we had only just passed the summer solstice, that was really saying something. I must've lost a couple of hours without even realizing it.

I looked over at Esja, still lost in her own work. There was a plate of food just by her elbow with a half-eaten cinnamon roll and the stems from a cluster of grapes. But it was scarcely surprising that her brother had nagged her into remembering to eat even as she painted.

Then I saw the plate of untouched food at my own elbow.

I looked back over my shoulder to see Loke apparently napping, slouched back in one of my comfy chairs with his hands folded on his belly. Mjolner was wrapped around his feet. I could hear the purring from across the room.

Loke opened a single eye when he felt me watching him. Then he winked, as much as saying that he'd told me so.

But I didn't care. I was covered in ink and my neck was aching from sitting too long hunched over my easel, but it felt wonderful.

For nearly three hours, I had stopped worrying about Thorbjorn, out on patrol with his brothers.

But that moment was gone now. And I was once more looking out that window, but not at what I wanted to draw. No, this time as I looked at the hills to the west, I wondered just where he was right at that moment.

And more than that, when he'd be home again.

CHAPTER TWO

I HAD to shoo Loke and Esja out before midafternoon. I felt a little bad about that, as Esja was still very engrossed in her work.

But I didn't need Loke to tell me she was pushing herself a little too hard. Her cheeks were mostly flushed with excitement, but not entirely. And she was working harder to keep her hands from trembling every time she raised her brush.

"She's going to crash as soon as we get home," Loke chided me in a low whisper as I walked them to my door.

"She's earned it," I whispered back. Then said to Esja, "I'll bring that painting down myself in the morning, or have someone bring it to you if I get caught up in volva duties."

"Okay," she said, chewing at her lip nervously. "But I'm not done with it."

"I know. It's just better to not try carrying it down that hill when it's wet."

"I know," she said, still chewing her lip. But then she pulled me into another hug. Not as strong as before, and with a bit more tremble in her arms this time, but still a welcome gesture.

"Heading off to Haraldr's?" Loke asked offhandedly as I followed them out the door and across my courtyard to the gate in my fence.

"Yes. That's the only reason I'd chase you both away, you know," I said.

"That's not the only reason," Loke said in a teasing drawl.

"No, I think it's probably at least reason number two," Esja said with a grin.

"Hey," I said, pretending to feel grumpier at being teased than I actually did. It was nice to see her having a moment with her brother.

But it's not like I needed a reminder that it had been twelve days since I'd seen Thorbjorn.

Twelve days, six hours, and... forty-two minutes.

Give or take.

"Which rune is it today?" Loke asked as we all stepped out onto the cobblestoned road and headed south, down the hill towards the end of town.

"Vend," I said. "It looks like if you made a capital P but with a triangle on top rather than a curve. It means joy and hope."

"If you know that already, why do you have to talk to Haraldr about it?" Esja asked.

If Loke had asked, I'd assume he was teasing me again. But Esja was sincerely asking.

"The letter shape and the translation are barely the surface of the thing," I told her. "There are more meanings, layers of them. And even then, learning all of it isn't the real work."

"What is?" she asked.

"I have to bond with it," I said, trying to explain a nebulous concept with hand gestures. Which wasn't illuminating at all, I was sure. I was mostly just describing round shapes and then waving my fingers around.

"She meditates on the rune," Loke said.

"Like when people in the east say 'om'?" Esja asked.

She might never have left Villmark a day in her life, but she was a voracious reader. Mostly of modern romances, but a few thicker tomes on weightier topics slipped in there from time to time.

"It's a little different," I said, although I had never attempted eastern meditation, so what did I know? But I gave it a shot. "I'm not so much trying to focus on one thing until I'm unfocused from everything, or focused on all things, or anything like that. I mean, it's not about the experience of meditation. It's more like... finding the relationship I already have with the concept that the rune represents."

"Huh," Esja said. I didn't blame her. I wasn't explaining it very well. But I'd never really tried to before. I just did it.

"I don't really feel a connection to any of the runes, but I don't feel a connection to that one in particular," Loke said, a shade too casually. Like he was trying to tell me something without saying it out loud. I gave him a questioning glance, but he just rolled his eyes in the direction of his sister.

Which was annoying. Why even bring it up if he didn't want to explain it?

I mean, aside from being something Loke did *all the time*.

But we had reached the point where our paths diverged. The two of them would continue on past the public gardens and greenhouses, then along the road through the pastures until they reached their Victorian house between the hills.

I, meanwhile, would turn in front of the gardens, following their northern edge past the council hall towards my favorite mead hall.

I mean, besides my grandmother's mead hall down in Runde, obviously.

Being one of the three members of the council, it made sense that Haraldr's house was here, close to where they met. But I had a feeling that the mead hall had also been a factor. Not that I ever saw Haraldr there, carousing with the youth. But I'd come inside his house on more than one occasion to smell the distinct combination of spices that Ullr always used on his roasted meat.

Not that anyone else could get takeout food from Ullr. But I suspected he made an exception for Haraldr.

"I'll see you tomorrow?" Esja asked, twisting the handles of her art bag in her hands as we stood at the crossroads.

"I hope so. But no promises," I said. "Something might come up."

"As if I would feel bad if it did," Esja scoffed at me. "I mean, exhibit number one of having something else come up is standing right next to me here."

She gave her brother a good-natured punch to the shoulder. But she was looking at me, so she didn't see the flash of real hurt in his eyes.

"Loke would never leave your side, if not being away was even a possibility," I told her sternly.

"I know that!" she laughed. "That's what I'm saying. I get it. More than responsibilities, you have things that literally pick you up and carry you away. I hope to see you tomorrow, but if I don't, I'll expect to hear the whole magical story when I *do* see you again. Deal?"

"Absolutely," I said. I gave her one last hug, but Loke was already walking away before I could even reach out to him.

Typical.

I turned to the left and followed the road east towards Haraldr's house.

Fulla, who tended his house for him, answered the door at my first knock, just as she always did. She had just celebrated her fourteenth birthday, and had had an impressive growth spurt to go with it. I would swear she was six inches taller than the last time I had seen her. Taller, and more willowy.

"Hello, Ingrid," she said with a smile as she stepped back to let me into the hall. "He's in the library, of course. He might be napping. I'd tell you not to wake him, but I don't think that's even possible."

"He's like a dragon in that way," I agreed. "He only looks like he's asleep. Sneak into his layer, and that eye is open and watching you."

"Exactly!" she laughed. "Do you need anything before you head in? I have some strawberries I picked from Haraldr's garden this morning and fresh cream?"

Tempting. But I had work to do.

"No, thanks, Fulla," I said. "I had company over for brunch, and I'm completely full."

I left her puzzling at how I could still be full from brunch at four in the afternoon—and she didn't even know how little of the food I had eaten—and headed down the corridor that ran like a spine down the center of Haraldr's house until I reached the first of the two doors into his library.

Haraldr was indeed sitting in a chair by the cold fireplace, hands folded over his belly, looking much like Loke had just an hour before. Well, a far older, balder Loke. But, also like Loke, he opened a single eye the moment he felt me looking his way.

"Oh, good, Ingrid," he said, and put both of his bony hands on the arms of his chair to push himself into sitting up straighter. "It is such a relief that the heat has passed, isn't it?"

"That, and the storms," I agreed as I settled into the chair opposite his by the fireplace. "I did so many drawings, sure that something supernatural was going on. But so far as I could tell, it was just weather."

"Sometimes weather is enough, if it's bad weather," Haraldr said. "And it will surely be miserably hot again before this summer is through. But I spent the morning out in the garden, watching Fulla pick strawberries. Well, she called it 'helping', but I don't think eating half of her haul is really helping."

"I'm sure she just meant your company was appreciated," I said.

Then I realized that was likely true. It must be lonely for Fulla, a girl her age basically holding down a more than full-time job. She was an orphan who had been taken in by the council when she was twelve, and moving into Haraldr's house to look after him had been her idea.

I knew because I had specifically asked. I had worked at a diner all through high school and beyond to pay for art school, because the income from my mother's job barely covered her ever-increasing medical expenses. I got having a strong work ethic even from a young age.

But I wondered if Fulla ever regretted it. I mean, I had made friends—one of them a lifelong friend—working at that diner. But Fulla was all alone, save for Haraldr.

I would have to find a way to ask her. Not that Haraldr could get by without someone around to look after him. But another helper or two to take some of the load off Fulla would doubtless be welcome.

A fourteen-year-old girl should have time to spend with other people her own age. And perhaps have fewer responsibilities.

"Something troubles you?" Haraldr asked as he smoothed the thin blanket that was draped over his knees.

"No, just making a mental note for later," I said. Because I wanted to talk to the woman on the council, Brigida, and also Fulla herself before I brought it up to Haraldr and the other council member, Thorbjorn's father, Valki.

"Somehow, I don't think it's art you're thinking of," he said with a merry gleam in his eye.

"No," I admitted. "But I did spend the last several hours thinking about art."

"I heard you had Esja over at your home," he said with a nod.

Of course, he had heard about that. For people who contended they preferred to keep to themselves, there was nothing slow about the Villmarker rumor mill.

And also, of course, he knew that thinking about art came after thinking about Esja.

But I was startled to hear him laughing.

"What?" I asked.

"Oh, the look on your face, dear," he said. "Such a guilty countenance for someone caught being generous with their time and themselves."

"I hardly paid attention to her when she was there," I admitted. And whatever he had seen in my face before, I really was feeling guilty now.

"If I know Esja, she was just pleased to be taken seriously as an artist, by a professional artist."

I couldn't exactly argue against that. Well, maybe the professional bit. I still owed my friend Jessica more ink illustrations to replace the ones she'd sold for me in her café.

"And this drawing you did during our recent storm. Were you worried about yourself, or about the town?"

"The town," I said, not quite adding the word *obviously*. "Loke and I still feel like there's a danger we don't understand that's on its way. But the storm wasn't it."

"Lose some sleep finding that out, did you?" he asked, in that teasing tone again.

"Yeah," I admitted, rubbing at my neck tiredly.

I watched as he pulled a little card out from under that blanket. A single character was drawn on it. The rune vend, just as I had described it to Esja.

"Joy and hope," I said, as I took the card from him and ran my fingertips over the rune.

"I almost don't think I need to explain this one to you," he said, settling back with his hands folded on his belly once more.

"I mean, that's pretty much all I know about it," I admitted.

"Joy is a virtue we strive for, as much as strength or generosity," he told me. "It means being joyful even as you work. Keeping your enthusiasm high, even when things get hard."

"I guess I try to do that," I said, but not with a lot of conviction. I felt like I failed as much as I succeeded. I felt overwhelmed, a lot. Like an impostor who only thought she could master magic, more than a lot.

But I worked to not let that show. That must be what Haraldr meant.

"Your art," he said, as if he knew I wasn't getting him. "You do the hard work, but you still bring that sense of finding the beauty to it. That's important. I think after spending the afternoon with Esja, you feel that even more than I can explain it to you."

"It's good to see her feeling happy," I said.

"But it's not just her you care about seeing happy," Haraldr said. "And it's not just the whole town. Because that's a concept it's easy to be too far removed from. You aren't working to protect Villmark, the idea of Villmark, safe. You're working to keep each individual person safe. And that means something more, you seeing them as individuals."

"Okay," I said, but I felt that guilty flush creeping back up on my cheeks. The truth was, there were people in Villmark I had to work hard to like.

But Haraldr was looking at me, not smiling or winking or anything like that, but with something in his eyes that told me he already knew that. And it was part of what he meant.

I looked at the rune in my hand again.

"Vend is the rune of fellowship. Of friendship and kin both. That isn't without its own sort of strife. But it's about holding strong together against the sorrows out there."

He gestured in a way that looked like he meant outside his windows. But I knew he meant the wilds outside of Villmark.

The ones the Thors were patrolling through in an endless quest to keep us all safe.

That was my mission, too. Just in a different way.

"I think I understand," I said, as I tucked the rune card into my sketchbook. "Of course, I often think that. Then the rune's true meaning blindsides me. So I know this is only the beginning of my work."

"Don't work too hard," Haraldr said, even as he slouched low in his chair, intent on continuing his nap. "Such a lovely day. And it's been so long since you've tended to your own stronghold."

"I've been in the family home in Villmark every day since the wedding," I said, confused.

"I meant *your* stronghold," he said, his eyes already closed. "Your little cabin in the woods."

"Oh, right," I said.

I hadn't forgotten about it, precisely. But it had been weeks and weeks since I'd been there. It was so remote from everything, so far from everyone in Villmark who might need me.

Then I saw Haraldr was looking at me again, like he was watching me figure him out. He gave me a wink, a wink that had just the faintest hint of a smirk to it.

Then he was napping for real. And I slipped out of the door without waking him.

CHAPTER THREE

IT WAS ABOUT five o'clock when I left Haraldr's house. Late afternoon in July, but the same time would be in darkness in a few short months. Despite not eating much at brunch, I wasn't particularly hungry. So rather than head home for dinner, I went east, to the meadow at the top of the waterfall that marked the border between Villmark behind its protective magic veil and the northern Minnesotan fishing town of Runde.

I wasn't in any particular hurry, and I was in a rather melancholy mood—not sad per se, just kind of quietly subdued—so I lingered in the meadow. The wildflowers were in full bloom, their scents blending pleasantly with the clean smell of sun-warmed grass.

But as lovely as that was, walking through the tall grass and dragging my fingertips over the nodding heads of the flowers, what I was truly focused on was the view beyond that field of blooms. The view that dominated the entire world to the east of Runde.

Lake Superior.

Even in July, its steel blue color looked cold. The breeze that danced through my hair wasn't exactly chilly, but it was cooler and smelled of the lake. I was standing at the very edge of the ridge, close enough to the waterfall for random gusts to blow water vapor over me in a fine mist.

I could see why my Viking era ancestors settled here. It had a more daunting beauty in the middle of winter, to be sure. But my ancestors had come from an island off the coast of Norway. Winter had never been anything they hadn't been quite prepared to deal with.

I wasn't sure why winter was so much on my mind that day. Maybe it was Haraldr's suggestion of taking time off and going to my cabin in the woods. It was a tempting idea.

But it felt like a dangerous temptation.

I could feel something coming, something darker and colder than winter. And taking a vacation was not going to prepare me to face it when it came.

I kind of wanted to talk to Loke about it. But that would have to wait at least another day. After all the excitement in the morning, Esja would need a quiet evening at home. And I knew there would be no dragging him away from her short of life-threatening peril.

What I worried about would still be there in the morning, and only a little bit closer for all my worrying. So I pushed it from my mind and headed back to the opening to the caves that tunneled deep throughout the bluffs behind the waterfall.

This system of caves was where the people of Villmark kept the few prisoners that were too dangerous to allow closer to the village. I had no idea how many there were all told, but I knew a growing number of them had been put there after I had exposed their crimes.

It didn't make for a comfortable walk. Even though my path didn't descend so deep as to where the cells were kept, I still sensed their presence as I left warm sunlight behind.

Or maybe it was just Halldis I sensed. She had some access to magic, although my skills were growing to a point I felt sure I would soon surpass her.

And she had never held a candle to my grandmother.

But she had used that magic to kill, and to trick others into helping her get away with her crimes.

And she hated me. I knew that for a fact.

I knew my magical protections were strong enough now for her to be no danger to me, locked in her cell as she was. But I still didn't feel entirely comfortable until I reached the larger cavern where we kept the sacred fire, the fire that fueled the protective magical barrier.

The fire we never let go out.

As I stepped into that cavern, I looked to see who was guarding the flames. When I had first come to Villmark, this had been a duty that only the five Thors shared. But in the months since, when the wilds outside of Villmark had become more and more of a danger, that duty had been extended to others. Like my friend Kara and her sister Nilda. Kara was still honeymooning with her new husband Thorge, but it was possible Nilda would be on duty.

But as I drew closer to the flames, I saw it was the Thors' father Valki who sat on the three-legged stool by the fire, sharpening a pair of hand-axes.

"Hello, Valki. Any news?" I asked, more out of politeness than anything. He was one of the three members of the high council, and so was privy to all the information that mattered in Villmark. But my days of being treated as an outsider were over. If there had been any news to report, someone would've sent me a missive.

"Thorbjorn and Frór are among the trolls, but they are holding the peace," he said. "Thormund is briefly at home, eating and sleeping around the clock, but he heads west again in the morning. Thoralv and Thorulv are on their way up from the south, but I'm not sure where they are precisely."

He didn't look up at me as he made this report, just continued honing his axe blades to a fine point. He tested one against the pad of his thumb, frowned, then went back to sharpening it with his stone.

"Are you worried about any of them?" I asked. "I can always send Mjolner with a message, you know."

"No, all is as it should be," he said. Then he paused in his sharpening to look up at me. "Heading down to see your mormor?"

"I am," I said. I realized I was holding the card with the vend rune drawing on it in my hands and slid it into my art bag.

"Nilda is coming soon to relieve me," he said. "Tell your grandmother I'll be down to see her this evening. I have a few things to discuss with her."

"Nothing serious, I hope?" I said.

"No, not serious," he said. His tone made it very clear that, while it might not be serious, it was definitely personal.

"I'll let her know," I said. Then gave him a wave before heading past the stone that was on occasion used to close the passage out. We seldom had need to use it, as the magic kept intruders from even finding this passage, but better safe than sorry.

I passed through the cave behind the waterfall. The air here was damp and cool, the sandy cave floor always wet and almost clayey.

Then I climbed the steep path down the bluffs, following the river until I reached the back of the building that, being that it was still daylight, looked like a recently renovated multipurpose building. The aluminum siding was freshly painted and showed not a hint of damage from ice or hail. The roof was new as well, the tiles as yet untouched by the inevitable crushing mounds of snow.

I let myself in the back door, into the space that looked like something between a meeting room and a bar. Which was what it was. The locals would hang out here like in a bar, but it was also used for the small government functions that Runde required from time to time.

After sunset, this place would look very different. The magic would come to life, and everyone inside would feel like they were inside a Viking era long house complete with wooden tables and benches, fire pits of roasting meat, and barrels of ale constantly on tap. Even the Runde locals would see it, although thanks to those same spells, they would never remember it once they left. Many of them had close Villmarker friends that, if pressed, they would say lived in the next town over. Even if the Villmarker in question was one of the traditionalists who never wore anything like modern Minnesotan clothing.

Currently, there were four men sitting together around a single table, drinking from bottles of mass-produced beer. I recognized them all as farming Sorensens, although I'd have been hard pressed to recall their first names. They all looked exhausted as they sat in silence. Like they'd agreed to go out for a beer after doing some labor-intensive chore and weren't going to back out on it now even though not a one of them was still feeling up for it.

Beyond that meeting room, closer to the front of the building, was the actual bar where my grandmother served the mead she brewed in the cellar below. But most of the front space was taken up by a general store that also served as the Runde post office.

My grandmother used to run all of this all by herself, but when she was forced to close for months after nearly collapsing from exhaustion—the magical kind—she had finally agreed to hire a little help. So it was Keith Sorensen sitting behind the counter when I came in. He had a couple of clipboards on the counter before him and seemed to be doing some sort of inventory, but still gave me a smile and a wave as I came in.

"She's down below," he told me.

"Thanks," I said, even as those words filled me with trepidation.

I had been in the cellar before, and I knew there was nothing down there but the barrels of mead and all the mead-making equipment my grandmother used.

But perhaps you can tell from my vagueness, I never really felt like that was a place I should be poking around in. It was my grandmother's private place, and I was loath to intrude.

Luckily, I didn't have to. Even as I drew near, the door before me swung open and my grandmother came in with her arms full of bottles of mead. I rushed forward to take some from her, then pushed the door closed behind her with her hip.

"Hello, Ingrid," my grandmother said with a smile as she set bottle after bottle onto the counter of her bar. Then she started taking the bottles out of my arms.

She had been drawn-looking for a long time after she had overtaxed her magic months before. And then, after opening the mead hall back up the month before, she had overtaxed herself again.

But she was back to full strength now, with a pink bloom to her cheeks that was heartening to see. Her long silver braid swung behind her as she spun to fetch something off the shelf behind her bar.

Even more heartening, she lifted a finger as if a sudden thought struck her, and I felt a magical twinge as she adjusted something in the spells that suffused the walls around us. Such a little gesture of almost no effort, but I felt the adjustment she had just made strongly.

"How is your new cabin coming?" I asked her when she turned back to me. Because I knew she never wanted to talk about how she was feeling if she could help it, so there was no point in asking about *that.*

"Oh, about as well as anyone would expect," she said with a smirk. "It's taking twice as long, and will surely cost nearly twice as much by the time they're done. But they've finished the river stone fireplace, if you wanted to go take a look."

"As long as it's sound by winter, that's the important thing," I said. I didn't like the idea of my grandmother spending the winter in the mobile home in the meeting hall parking lot. Her magic needed the focus of hearth and home, and despite having the word "home" in it, that mobile home was not cutting it.

"I've been giving them what aid I can," she said. "Not that there was anything I could do about that storm."

She shuddered at the memory.

"I looked, lots of times, but all I ever saw was normal weather," I said.

"Oh, yes. Nothing magical there," she agreed. Then she gave me a sly little look. "Did you think I'd done something to draw that down?"

"Not remotely," I said. "Why would you make it *storm?*"

"Well, we both know how good magical intentions can often go so very far awry," she said.

"I suppose. But that wasn't what worried me," I said.

"No, I guess I know what did worry you," she agreed. Then she was giving me another twinkling-eyed look. "Too many things worry you, Ingrid. It's not healthy for you."

"Nothing I'm worried about is anything that isn't, by its nature, worrisome," I said.

"I know. I'm not saying I think you're being paranoid," she said. Then she leaned back against the shelf behind her, crossing her arms as she pinned her gaze on me. "No, I'm saying you could use a break from all the worrying. That's all."

"Have you been talking to Haraldr?" I asked suspiciously.

"Not specifically," she said, taking out a rag and wiping down her already spotless counter. "Why do you ask?"

"Because I was just at his house, and he suggested I take a vacation. He said I should spend some time in my cabin in the woods."

"Oh, that sounds like a marvelous idea," she said. "This is the perfect time to do it, too."

"How is this the perfect time?" I asked. My tone came out so miserable it almost sounded sulky. But all I could think was, how could it really be a vacation if Thorbjorn was so far away?

My grandmother was looking at me too intently again, and I rubbed at my face as if I could erase my own expression.

"I meant because it's the height of summer," she said almost sternly. "The things that come down from the north, they tend to cross over more in the depths of winter. I suspect the Wild Hunt gives them an opening as it passes through. Or they follow it. But summer is safer whatever the reason, I know that for a fact. Definitely safer to be alone."

"Why do I have to be alone?" I asked.

"Well, I guess I assumed that Mjolner would be with you," she said. "But at this point in your training, great quantities of time alone with your own thoughts is absolutely necessary. But don't think I don't remember how lonely that was. It was decades ago, but I remember it well."

I didn't answer. The truth was, I wasn't much less lonely living in the center of Villmark, surrounded by people. Being actually alone might perversely make me feel it less. Or I'd feel more at one with the forest. Or something.

But the idea was starting to grow on me.

"Everyone will know how to contact me if they need me, right?" I asked. I felt like I was offering the terms of my surrender.

But before my grandmother could answer, Valki strolled in from the back room. I hadn't even heard him come in through the door. But he had heard my words, because the first thing he said was, "Where are you going?"

"Ingrid is going to take a few days to herself in the cabin Solvi Ulfarrsen left for her out in the woods north of Villmark," my grandmother told him.

I bit my lip, too nervous to see how he would respond to this. But I suppose I shouldn't have been surprised when he enthusiastically agreed to this plan.

It was feeling more and more like the council had planned it out ahead of time. But not because they wanted to get me out of the way or anything like that.

No, to me, it felt more like they were really concerned that I was pushing too hard, taking on too many responsibilities. And rather than insisting I could handle it, I decided I would, indeed, take a vacation.

I remembered all too well the sight of my grandmother after she had pushed too hard. And as much as I didn't think I was pushing anywhere near that hard, I could respect that the council would feel better about things if they could see me taking a break.

And, like my grandmother had said, this was the perfect time. With Thorbjorn far to the north, I had nowhere better to be.

Because, of course, that cabin was ever so slightly closer to where he was.

CHAPTER FOUR

THREE DAYS LATER, I was really glad I had agreed to take a vacation.

As much as it didn't really feel like a vacation.

I mean, I had fallen in love with that cabin in its own clearing in the woods from the moment I had set eyes on it. A little round house with a bright green door, with a little kitchen garden on the south side, a well in the back, and gorgeous wooden carvings arranged like all the woodland creatures were having a party. And every board that the cabin was constructed from was gently carved and lovingly stained to bring out the patterns in the wood that most evoked the waters of the lake that was ever-present in all our minds, even if it was out of sight in this hollow deep in the woods.

And I had only fallen deeper in love when I had first seen the elaborately carved details of its interior. It was all one round room save for a tiny bathroom addition on the north side. The elaborate carved knot work that graced all the wood beams had been painted in shades of red, blue and gold to make the patterns pop.

The bed was like an ornate magic box, with carvings of wolves chasing the sun and moon, and a more elaborate representation of the founding of Villmark centuries before, only visible to those lying on the mattress and looking up.

The fireplace had carvings for each of the nine worlds in Norse cosmology. They were a little harder to see because of smoke damage from the sadly necessary fireplace, but still lovely all the same.

But my favorite thing remained Yggdrasil, the world tree, which formed the central beam that rose up to the tallest point of the domed roof above. There were all the details of dragons, eagles, and squirrels from the old stories, nestled among delicately carved branches and even more delicate suggestions of the leafy canopy.

The kitchen had scenes of food gathering from the old days, and even the bathroom had a scene of Valkyries riding off to collect the souls of the battle-dead.

It was all, quite simply, almost too gorgeous to live in.

But there were some things I hadn't noticed when I was there before.

Well, there were a lot of things I hadn't noticed when I was there before.

I mean, the structure itself was in good shape. I didn't need to try my hand at repairing a thatched roof or anything like that.

But the kitchen area had needed the most epic of scrubbings, because something I didn't want to dwell too long on was growing over all the surfaces.

I really hoped it wasn't black mold. But even if it was, my combination of modern world cleaners with a little magic of my own would definitely be enough to eradicate it. I just combined the earthy elements of Ur with a little Fe fire. And a dash of Kaun, just to be sure. Although that felt like taking the nuclear option.

But, as I said, I was sure my kitchen was clean. And whatever film that had been discoloring everything, it would never return.

I aired out the rest of the little cabin for good measure. The last time I had touched Thurs energy, I had summoned the out-of-season tornado that had picked up my grandmother's previous cabin then dashed it to the ground again. But I was more careful this time, just getting a strong breeze to swirl through the round, single-room interior until every corner was dust- and cobweb-free.

The bedding Solvi had left behind I just tossed into the fire pit. I don't want to make any assumptions about bachelors who are artist-types, but I had no shortage of bedding back at my house in Villmark. I just preferred to sleep in my own sheets, under my own duvet.

Mjolner stayed with me all through this work, even though it was exactly the kind of upheaval he generally preferred to make himself scarce from. Perhaps if I had pulled out a vacuum cleaner, he would've scattered. But magical winds were nothing he feared.

I also kind of suspect he was keeping an eye on me. But who was he reporting to? My grandmother? The high council? Loke? Thorbjorn?

If I had to make a guess, I'd say all the above. But I didn't mind. It was kind of nice to have the support of people who gave me my space, but were also always there for me. It wasn't something I would ever take for granted.

By the end of the third day, I had the entire place spotless. More than that, it was starting to have a smell that felt like *my place*. I can't explain exactly what that smell is. It's not like my body odor or anything gross like that. It was more like the sheets smelled like *my* laundry soap and the kitchen smelled of *my* favorite foods.

And the whole place definitely smelled like a small cabin where a cat lived. But I had never minded that smell myself. Cat people usually don't. After it becomes part of the smell of your place, you don't even notice it anymore, really.

And Mjolner always did his business outside, anyway. Outside, and far from the garden. Sometimes it was handy, having a cat who could walk through walls.

I woke up the fourth morning with the idea of starting a little art, maybe finally getting around to bonding with the vend rune like I was supposed to. But when my morning tea was ready, I took the mug with me as I strolled through the forest clearing that was, for all intents and purposes, my yard.

It was filled with wooden sculptures that Solvi had left behind. They were gorgeous creations, real animals, but also things that most people would think of as fairy creatures or mythological beings. I had admired his work even before I had met him.

And I still admired it, even after I had been forced to sentence him to banishment to the north. He had been a murderer, after all. Not the worst murderer I had ever met—no, those were all in the cells in the deeper caves behind the waterfall—but a murderer all the same.

But the heart that had carved these statues hadn't nursed that destructive tendency. They looked like he had tried to bring something to life, truly and passionately.

And in that moment, as I sipped my tea and felt the rising sun ever warmer on my skin, I knew those almost-living sculptures had a job they were longing to do.

They wanted to house protective magics. And after months of helping my grandmother with the spells that protected the mead hall, I knew just what to weave through them and around them to protect my snug little cabin.

I had to move some of the statues around as I wove the spells. This bear needed to be closer to those gnomes but farther from the wolf, things like that. Not that there were any kind of rules written down anywhere. It was just an intuition I had as I worked. I could feel it as the web of spells around me grew stronger, and I knew my instincts were right.

And also that I had to admit my grandmother had been completely correct. This time alone with my magic was exactly what I needed at this point in my education. I mean, Haraldr had mentioned the concept of bind runes, but he had never taught me how to pick which runes to combine, or how to draw the power together.

Because while Haraldr had read every book in the world about runes and their meanings, he had no access to magic himself. He could never actually *do* anything with them. He couldn't even really sense them the way I did.

Yes, this time alone, sorting things out and just feeling things was just what I hadn't known I needed. I had so much left to learn, and I knew it. But it was nice to take a moment and realize just how far I'd come already.

I couldn't protect all of Villmark, not yet. Not the way my ancestress Torfa had. But I was doing a fine job protecting my own little cabin.

I mean, I could tell Mjolner was impressed. And he was a cat. Do you have any idea how hard it is to impress a cat?

I spent another three days just on those wards. Luckily, the fine weather held on. It stayed warm but not too hot, with puffy clouds scattered over the sky but never any sign of rain. And if there'd been anything like the humidity from before the storm, I never would've been able to haul all those wood sculptures around by myself. Not without passing out from the heat.

Then I woke on the seventh day alone with Mjolner in that cabin. I made my morning tea, poured it into my mug, then once again walked out into the clearing around the cabin. But there was nothing more to be done out there. All the sculptures were perfectly arranged. The wards that protected the clearing and cabin both stood strong. Strong yet invisible to the senses of magic creatures.

Having briefly been a beacon of strong but uncontrolled magic, I knew the importance of not drawing more attention than I meant to well.

I went back into my cabin, that mug of tea still half-full in my hand, and looked around the interior. But there was no work left for me there either. Everything was arranged just as I liked it, everything was clean, and the kitchen was well-stocked.

I literally had nothing else to do.

So after the tea was gone, I took my easel out into the clearing, set a stool before it, and got out my charcoals.

I thought I was setting to work, finally ready to bond with my newest rune. But that wasn't all that happened. I started there, to be sure. But my hand and my mind became one, and my drawings ranged everywhere, incorporating every rune I had learned so far. So many overlaps and arrangements.

So very many meanings.

That set of three days blew by, all in one blur. I scarcely knew day from night. My meals certainly had no schedule. It was just me and the charcoal in my hand and the paper before me.

Under Mjolner's watchful eye, of course.

But I knew it was three days, because I'd long grown accustomed to just knowing that I was in a magical space, and in a magical space things came in threes. They just did.

So it was on sunset on the ninth day when I put the last fragment of charcoal stick back in the box under my easel and wiped my darkly powdered hands on a towel too black with charcoal already to be of any real use. I looked at all the pages I had filled. Four notebooks of eighteen by twenty-four inch pages. Densely filled.

But I didn't feel drained. I felt the opposite. I felt charged up.

But I also felt a little like I was expecting something. So when I packed everything up and brought it back into the house, sort of telling myself that I was going to wash up before making something actually substantive for dinner, I kind of knew those plans were never going to come to fruition.

And, indeed, the moment I had the easel sitting back in its spot between the canopied bed and the dining table just big enough for two, I glanced up out of the window.

There was a figure approaching out of the trees. I wasn't facing the path to Villmark. I was facing the other path, the one that led eventually to the north. To the hills where the trolls lived.

But I wasn't worried. I knew that lanky walk, that hunched posture that clung to the shadows, that dark silhouette.

Loke was coming to see me. And given how Loke traveled, almost completely at random, it wasn't that odd to see him coming from any direction at all.

But he usually traveled through doorways. I supposed he couldn't come directly through my cabin doorway, not just because I had warded everything, but also because his power was really not under his control most of the time.

Still, it was strange. How far had he walked to get to me? I couldn't even imagine where the nearest doorway was in that direction.

I looked down at my charcoal-covered hands, but just wiped them on my cutoffs as I headed to my doorway to meet him.

I could feel worry radiating off him in waves. I just didn't know what it was that was worrying him.

I only hoped it wasn't Esja.

CHAPTER FIVE

The first words out of Loke's mouth were, "It's not Esja. And it's not Thorbjorn either."

Followed immediately by, "Do you have anything to eat? I'm famished."

He was also still clearly worried, despite his dismissive attitude. But rather than press him before he was ready to talk, I just nodded and headed into my little kitchen. My substantive meal plans gave way to the simpler opening of a can of soup to be heated on the camp stove I had set on top of the cabin's wood-burning stove.

Because while the heat had broken for a bit, it was still too hot to run a wood-burning stove just to make dinner.

While it warmed up, I took a few rolls of rye bread out of my bread box, sliced some dark goat cheese to go with it, and added a few wedges of red and green apples.

When I had plated all this up and put it in front of Loke, he wolfed it down like he hadn't seen food in days.

Then I realized I was eating with impolite speed myself. I wasn't sure exactly what I had been eating while doing art over the last three days, but it definitely hadn't been much. And the sharpness of the cheese really brought out the sweetness in the apples.

Even the tinned chicken soup tasted improbably good. Hunger really is the best sauce.

"Okay, time for you to talk to me," I said as I divided the last soup remaining in the pan between our two bowls for seconds.

"Normally, this isn't the sort of thing that would bother me at all," he said as he dunked a chunk of rye roll into the broth and watched as the bread soaked it up. "Maybe that's the thing that's most worrying about all this."

"It's worrying because it's worrying?" I asked with a frown.

"Exactly," he said, as if relieved I understood him. Which I kind of did. If he had tried to shrug whatever this was off as not his problem, and had failed to stop thinking about it, that really was worrying.

I mean, no one is better at dismissing something from his mind than Loke.

"What's going on?" I asked. "You said it wasn't your sister."

"No, all parties in this matter are decidedly male. But not of the red-headed, hulking variety," he said, and popped the soup-soaked bread in his mouth.

"Go on," I said.

"You know they've beefed up the patrols close to Villmark, right?" he said around his mouthful of food. "The Thors and Frór are the only ones ranging further out, but a lot of the local men have volunteered to help keep watch closer to the village proper."

"Okay," I said. I had probably heard something like that in a council meeting. But there were so many details in those meetings, anything that didn't directly pertain to me tended to fall right back out of my mind again. "Do these patrols not include the outlying farms like yours?"

"No, but that's not what this is about," he said. "You don't need to worry about Esja and I, you know. As warded up as this place is—nice work, by the way—our ancestral home has its own far more impressive protections."

"I've never noticed that," I said. His house still had rooms that showed the smoke and flame damage from the fire that had killed his parents. The entire place creeped me out more than a little.

But huge magic, like he was talking about? I should've noticed that.

"You will, someday," Loke said with a dismissive wave. "I've told you my magic is different than yours, remember? But that's not important now."

"Okay, go on," I said, but reluctantly. Loke was just too good at deflecting my questions. Mostly because what he deflected me to was always something I really needed to be paying more attention to at the moment.

And my gut was already telling me this was one of those moments.

"The patrol?" I prompted.

He soaked up the last of his soup with the last chunk of bread and chewed and swallowed. Then he set the bowl away from him as if to remove a temptation. Only then did he start to speak.

"There is one field in particular, north and west of my house, south and west of Villmark proper, on top of a hill, but not a particularly tall hill."

"I'm guessing this is a place you can just point out to me?" I asked.

"Sure, but what I'm saying now is that this place is within the farmlands south of Villmark. Outside the village, sure, but this should still definitely be considered within the zone of safety. I mean, it's inside the area that's being patrolled the most heavily."

"What's been happening on this hill?" I asked.

"It started two nights ago, although I only heard any of this just a few hours ago myself," he said. "It involves the patrols themselves, so I'm a little annoyed that you don't seem to have any clue what I'm talking about."

"I told the council to contact me if they needed me," I said. It took a real effort to get the next words out and sound like I meant them, but I did it. "If they didn't call me, I would have to conclude they felt they didn't need me."

"Hmph," Loke said, clearly unimpressed. "Well, let's be the judge of that in a minute."

"Two nights ago, what happened?" I asked.

"Two nights ago, while crossing that field on the hilltop, an entire patrol just disappeared," he said.

"What do you mean, disappeared? Did anyone see this happen? I mean, how do you know it was crossing this field?"

"They were seen crossing the road and climbing that hill, and they were never seen coming down the other side," Loke said with a shrug.

"Who were they?" I asked, just barely not asking if they were anyone I knew.

"They were all young, like twenty tops. Dagr, Niáll and Odkel by name," he said.

I repeated the names to myself, but in the end had to shake my head. Although I wasn't sure I could name any people that age from Villmark. I might know them by sight, though.

"They've only been patrolling for two weeks. Raw recruits, I do have to wonder why they were all together on the same patrol," he said.

"Rather than mixed with more experienced patrollers? I don't know," I said. Although I agreed it was worrying.

"They never checked in, but I don't know if anyone seriously started searching for them until the next night," Loke said. "Because waiting past sundown is just the best way to find missing people, don't you think?"

I wasn't sure that sarcasm was any more helpful than the waiting had been, but opted not to call him out on it. "What happened last night?" I asked instead.

"Another patrol went out, following the same route," he said. "But they were walking the usual patrol and looking for the lost three at the same time."

"You do realize we don't exactly have an abundance of volunteers for this duty?" I reminded him.

"I'm hardly going to complain when I'm not willing to step up myself," he said. He was smirking, but I knew he was far from joking when he added, "I mean, if I go out on patrol, who's going to watch out for my sister?"

"Me," I said. "Nilda. Sigvin. We'd all be happy to have her, here in town."

"Here in town?" He repeated, the smirk turning up a notch. "Ingy, we're not *in* town."

"Point taken," I said. "Which is why I gave you two of what is likely more than a dozen willing backups."

"Whatever," Loke said with another dismissive wave. "Can I go on with my story?"

"Please."

"So last night, Raggi, Skefill and Yngvi were on the patrol looking for the first three," he said. "I know you know who they are."

"Yes, I do," I said. Raggi and Skefill I had crossed paths with more than once while investigating murders. They were what was known as Villmarker isolationists, people who thought that Runde was an evil temptation that should be forbidden to all Villmarkers.

Needless to say, we hadn't really gotten along.

But they had never been guilty of the crimes I had been investigating, although they had definitely been far too possible as suspects.

Yngvi I knew less well, but he was married to one of the Freyas, sisters who were cousins to the Thors.

Two of the Freyas had been taken by the Wild Hunt before I had found the man who was luring them out of safety during the darkest nights of winter. I still hated that I hadn't caught him sooner, that I hadn't saved their lives.

Yngvi's wife hadn't been one of the victims. But I think it was still safe to say Yngvi was not what you would call an Ingrid Torfudottir fan.

"I'm guessing they've disappeared as well," I said, rubbing at my forehead. Luckily, I had washed the charcoal off my hands properly before I had started dinner.

"Last seen crossing the same road, climbing the same innocuous hilltop," Loke said.

"I can see why I'm worried about this," I said. "But what's bothering you about it? I mean, I don't think you're wrong. This isn't the kind of thing that usually bothers you. I'm pretty sure you don't feel any fondness for any of these men."

"I like people," he said with feigned defensiveness.

"Too close to your home?" I asked, not willing to let him deflect me with humor this time.

"Three and three," he said. "Like you said, we only have so many volunteers. How many nights can we stand to lose another three young men? And no one is even calling the Thors back."

"I might chalk it up to warm summer nights and young men bored of their duties—" I started to say.

"If not for Yngvi," Loke finished for me with a nod.

"Right," I said grimly.

Well, my vacation was over. It had been nice while it lasted.

"I really hope this doesn't mean six murders," I said, and looked at him intently to see how he would react.

He just shrugged. "I don't think so. I looked all over that hilltop before I came here, and I didn't see any signs of blood or of a fight. Lots of trampled grain, but nothing cut with a blade or anything."

"Magic?" I asked, my voice almost a croak as I choked on the word.

But to my relief, he was shaking his head again. "No, none of that, either. Honestly, the lack of clues is part of what's so worrying about it. I don't know what's going on. But I want to. Which appears to make me unique, as the council doesn't seem to be *doing* anything about it."

"Well, it often looks that way from the outside, even when it's very different on the inside," I told him.

"I'm never going to be on the inside," he said, but not with any particular bitterness. Loke preferred to be outside things. Even if caring for his sister and the bizarre nature of his power didn't keep him isolated, I was pretty sure that would still be true.

"I should take a look at that hilltop," I said, and started looking around for my art bag.

"Absolutely," Loke agreed. "But first you need to talk to the council."

"I'd rather have some evidence to give them that they don't already have before I go making any demands," I said.

"Like you ever make demands of them," Loke scoffed. "But seriously, I'm taking you to the council first."

"You're taking me," I repeated skeptically.

"There's a doorway right there," he said, gesturing to my front door.

"I'm sorry, but what was tripping me up was the part about you taking me to the *council*," I said. "You hate the council."

"I'm not talking to them. You are," he said.

"Loke—" I started to say.

But in a flash he was around the table, grasping my upper arms so I would focus on him and not the art bag that I was positive I had left right there when I had come in from outside.

"Listen, this is me telling you. We need to bring in the Thors for this. Something is close that shouldn't be close, and we need them here."

I blinked at him. I couldn't remember the last time I had seen him so earnestly serious. It shook me.

But I still had to ask. "What's close?"

"I don't know," he said, letting me go to clench his fists in frustration. "I just know it's close. And I don't want you going anywhere near it without a Thor beside you. Preferably Thorbjorn, but I guess any Thor in a pinch."

"All right," I said, as soothingly as I could. "Let me get my bag and we'll go."

"You have to convince them," he said even as he went to the doorway to wait for me.

I shoved a fresh set of pencils and a new sketchbook inside my bag, then slung it over my shoulder.

"I will," I promised him, clutching the strap of my bag in a way that I hoped showed my own earnest seriousness.

But the minute he turned towards the door, I looked back over my shoulder at Mjolner.

Mjolner gave me a slow wink of one green eye. I thought it was a "go get 'em" gesture of solidarity.

But I kind of hoped it was also a promise that if the council didn't agree with Loke's plan, Mjolner and I were of a mind on what we'd do next.

Which was to totally bring the Thors in ourselves.

But I hoped it didn't come to that. Things had been going so well. I was accepted as a part of the community. It really wasn't the time to start throwing my weight around.

But I would if I had to.

CHAPTER SIX

THE DOORWAY LOKE chose for us to emerge from was in the back of the hall of the high council, the door from their storage pantry into the kitchen area where they took more casual meetings.

I had been here before, but it was no less a startling sight than it had been that first time. I knew I was standing in a room tucked behind the dais of the grand Viking style hall where the high council held court. But, as much as that space was pure Norse woodwork with a worn stone floor and lit only by firelight from braziers, this place behind the heavy curtain that was always draped closed behind the three stools on that dais was nothing like that at all.

No, it was just a typical northern Minnesotan kitchen, if a few decades out of date. The refrigerator opened with a long horizontal handle that needed to be tugged quite forcefully to get it open. The avocado green color still suggested a lack of modern safety features in that unit, because while fashions came and went, that color had never cycled back into popularity.

The gas stove beside it was a lurid shade of harvest gold, another color that had already had its day.

But the formica table with its blue flowers on a white background was still rather charming, if a bit chipped from use.

And around that table sat the high council. Valki, not on duty at the ancestral fire or on patrol despite all that was apparently happening, sat on the left. Haraldr, currently blowing steam off of a mug of tea he held in ever so slightly shaking hands, was on the right.

And in the center sat Brigida, with her beringed-hands wrapped around a mug of her own. Her thick silver hair was done up in a crown braid, as tidy as ever.

And directly in front of me was a fourth empty chair with a plate and mug set before it. Like they were waiting for me.

I really shouldn't have been surprised that they appeared to have been waiting for me.

Or that, the minute I stepped out of the pantry door, it slammed shut behind me. Leaving me alone, without Loke.

Well, he did avoid the council as much as he could.

"Sorry to interrupt," I said with a nervous smile.

"Nonsense," Brigida said, gesturing to the plate in the center of the table. "Have some butter cookies and tea while we discuss everything."

"Aren't we waiting for Mormor?" I asked.

"No," Valki said. "She's been informed, but she has left the decisions on this up to us."

"You three or we four?" I asked.

Brigida didn't answer. She just gave me that gentle smile of hers.

I sat down and let her pour out a cup of tea for me. But I didn't reach for a cookie.

It didn't feel like any of us should be in a cookie mood.

"I see it was young Loke Grímsson who brought you here through our pantry, but was he also the one who sent for you? Or was it your cat?" Haraldr asked between sips of tea.

I took a sip of my own. Minty, but with a hint of citrus. At least caffeine wouldn't be keeping me up all night.

"It was Loke," I said. "These disappearances happened very near his home. He's worried about his sister."

"Aren't we all," Brigida said mildly. Although the council even being aware of her existence was news to me. "We do wish he'd move her into town. Especially as he is as convinced as you are that we are all in danger."

"You don't think we are?" I asked, almost choking on the little tea I had in my mouth.

"Of course we believe you," Haraldr said, putting a bony hand on mine. "It's just a matter of how much time we're talking about. Danger could be imminent in months, years, or decades. Runic foretellings are notoriously vague about such details."

"I feel like it's close," I said.

"As does your grandmother," Valki said. "But we can't keep the entire village on high alert indefinitely."

"Who said anything about indefinitely?" I asked. "You *are* aware that six men are missing?"

"We are," Valki said.

"And yet no high alert?" I asked.

"My sons are on it," Valki said. "That is sufficient."

"Which sons?" I quickly asked.

Too quickly, he seemed to think, to judge from the smallest of smirks. But he answered me seriously. "Thoralv and Thorulv were closest, so they are investigating. The other local patrols have been sent to the north and west for now, for their own safety. My sons will watch that field on the hilltop from sunset to sunrise, then report to us what they've learned."

"And if they get taken too?" I asked.

"Do you think that's likely?" Brigida asked me. Her tone was mild, but her eyes on mine were uncomfortably intent.

I chewed at my lip but forced myself to carefully consider my answer before I gave it.

"All five of them were taken once, as well as Frór," I reminded them all. Although that had happened when all six of them were very far north of Villmark, towards the mountains of Old Norway.

"Is that the danger you sense now? So close to us? That thing that held them trapped in nightmares?" Haraldr asked.

I closed my eyes and reached out with my senses. The field in question was only a ten-minute walk from where we sat around the formica table. I extended my magical senses beyond that point, past Loke's house to the south and equally far to the west, into the uninhabited woods.

But in the end, I had to admit I felt nothing. "No, but I think I'll take a stroll over that hill just to be sure."

"We did send you away to rest for a purpose, you know," Haraldr said.

"You sent me away?"

"Invited you to take a break, then," Valki amended. "We need you rested up. We need you ready."

"For?"

"Anything," he said.

"We can't put the village on high alert, as Valki has said," Brigida said, taking a cookie from the platter and setting it on the little plate in front of her. But she only brushed crumbs off its surface, a fussy little gesture. "You and the Thors, we do need you all at high alert. But high alert at all times, that is exhausting. Don't think for a minute we don't recognize that."

"We have my sons on a rotation," Valki said. "Always one at home."

"I got the sense that was more for Gunna's benefit than for theirs," I said.

He flushed a little, but just shrugged. "It achieves two purposes. After her sister lost two of her daughters, you can hardly blame her for being nervous about her own sons."

"We're all nervous for your sons," Brigida said, putting a hand on his forearm and giving it a gentle squeeze.

"We'd put Loke on high alert as well, if we thought we could get his cooperation in such a thing," Haraldr said.

"You don't need to worry about that," I said. "Loke is on higher alert than anybody. I mean, he's the one who came to tell me about what was going on."

"He might be on too high of an alert," Valki grumbled under his breath.

"I appreciate knowing what's going on," I said. "Look, I get that you want me resting and preparing. And if you tell me the Thors have this under control, I'm certainly not going to argue. But I appreciate being kept in the loop. I might perceive things that the three of you do not. And I can't believe I still have to point that out to you."

"Your grandmother walked over the hill this afternoon," Brigida said. "She felt nothing. No hint of residual magic or trace of a creature that should not be seen so close to the village."

"She said it was like the six missing men just walked away," Valki said.

"Fine, as far as that goes, but I've explained to you all about those women from the north. The ones that—and I hate to point this out again—took all five of your sons as well as Frór and held them captive for months. These six men are no more likely to resist their charms if tested, surely."

I realized I was raising my voice, which hadn't been my intention. But rather than apologize for it, I crossed my arms and waited for their response.

"Your grandmother has had experience with at least one of these women as well, yes?" Brigida said.

"She was looking for signs of them specifically," Haraldr told me. "She didn't find any."

I chewed at my lip. I didn't want to ever imply that I could see things that my grandmother couldn't. I was all too aware that her power was at a level I was decades away from even approaching.

And yet I knew my mind wouldn't rest easy until I looked for myself.

"As a favor to Loke, I'm just going to stroll over that hilltop," I said at last. "I won't get in the way of whatever Thoralv and Thorulv are doing, I promise. I'll be back in my cabin before sunset. But I *am* going to take a look."

"At least have a cookie before you go," Haraldr said, taking one off the platter and sliding it onto the plate before me.

"One for the road," I said, getting up from the table with my tea untouched after that first sip. I picked up the cookie and slipped it into my pocket. Then, with a nod to each of them, I headed out into the darkened interior of the hall, then out the huge double doors to the street beyond.

Where I found Mjolner waiting for me, perched on a fence post outside the public garden on the far side of the street, washing his ears in the light of the setting sun.

"Shall we?" I said to him.

He hopped down from the fence post, falling into step beside me.

We followed the main road as it ran straight past the public gardens and greenhouses. Then it grew narrower and more meandering, weaving a path between the rolling hills that were dotted with grazing cows.

I knew at once which hill I was looking for. Not that Loke's description had been so fantastic. I just had a gut sense.

This was a place where something had happened.

But as I walked through the tall grass, here and there clipped shorter by the grazing herds, I had to admit that I agreed with my grandmother's assessment.

I sensed nothing magical around me. No traces of power, no lingering scents from trolls, not even a trampling of the grass to show signs of a fight.

And yet I found the place… unquiet. Like I was standing where a battle had once been fought, centuries before.

Which maybe it had. Only I had passed this hill before, many times, on my way to and from Loke's house. And I had never felt anything like that before.

I sat down on the grass and Mjolner came up to sit beside me. I put a hand on his back and felt the rumble of his purring breath.

"What do you think?" I asked him.

He looked up at me with those intelligent green eyes, and I felt like he almost wanted to talk to me.

But the words didn't come.

"Maybe it's time to just go home," I said. "Maybe if I meditate before bed, I'll get some clues in a dream. That's happened before."

Mjolner meowed dismissively. Or maybe skeptically. It was hard to tell.

"Do *you* sense anything?" I asked.

He looked around like he was scanning the horizon, taking in Villmark on the taller hills to the north, the tree-covered hills that piled up ever higher to the west, and the lower, field-covered hills to the south.

Then he looked up at me and winked one eye very slowly.

"There *is* something, isn't there?" I mused, as much to myself as to him. "But it isn't anything I've ever felt before. And it doesn't exactly feel dangerous, does it?"

He winked at me again.

And this time I thought I did know what he was saying. He was agreeing with me. This strange thing didn't feel dangerous.

But sometimes that was the most dangerous thing of all.

CHAPTER SEVEN

THAT NIGHT, with Mjolner curled up and purring against the back of my neck, I slept particularly deeply. But if I had any dreams, I didn't remember them.

Although that might have been because of how I was woken up, by a panicked pounding on my cabin door. Any fragment of a dream that might have lingered was scattered by the sudden jacking up of my heart rate.

I threw back the covers and ran to the window first. The sun might have risen over the waters of Lake Superior, but it had not yet gotten high enough to appear through the trees in my home in the valley north of Villmark.

I also couldn't see who was at the door from that window. I only knew that whoever it was, they hadn't triggered any of the protective wards.

But was that a good thing or a bad thing?

I was still hesitating when the pounding came again. This time followed by a voice calling through the thickness of the door, "Ingrid Torfudottir? Let me in. It's Thorulv Valkisson."

Well, that answered *that* question. My wards had nothing to fear from a Thor. I ran to throw open the door. The tall man on the other side pushed past me to get inside as if Odin's hounds of the Wild Hunt themselves were after him.

I closed the door, then turned to see him still standing, lingering uncertainly in the middle of my living area. He was twisting his hands together, over and over again. He was the oldest of the five brothers, although still not quite thirty. His long beard—long enough that he wore it tucked under the crossbody straps that held his weapons—was the same reddish-gold color they all shared, but he kept his head shaved. It had been a while since I had been close enough to him to properly see the blue tattoos that were woven in an intricate pattern over his scalp, but this time I was able to pick out a few bind runes I recognized. Runes of strength and protection.

He had both his swords and both his hand axes arranged around the leather crossbody straps.

But what he didn't have was a brother with him.

"Where's Thoralv?" I asked. Not that I was really worried yet. They were on patrol together, but Valki had said they would be watching only until sunrise, and it was just sunrise now. Perhaps he had come after his shift was done to see me about… whatever he was here to see me about.

But the sudden look of anguish on his face, the one he immediately tried to hide by covering that face with both his calloused hands, worried me deeply.

"Thorulv? What happened?" I asked, even as I caught him by both arms and directed him to sit in the nearest chair. I couldn't have reached his shoulders to do this if I'd tried, but he let himself be guided by me.

I sat down opposite of him and waited for him to take those hands off his face. I didn't think he was crying, but I deeply suspected he was battling the impulse even as I watched.

"I don't know what's happened," he said at last, his voice muffled from behind his hands.

Then he dropped them. His face was splotchy, and his eyes were red-rimmed, but both were dry.

"But you came here," I said, even as I reached for my art bag. I was going to need paper and pencils. I just knew it.

"I *ran* here," he said. "I ran all the way here. But now I've forgotten why."

The look in his blue eyes made my heart quake. It was such an agony of despair, but also with a hope that I was going to fix everything.

"Tell me what you do remember," I said as I opened my sketchbook. "Anything at all. Images, fragments. Whatever you can recall. Don't try to force any memories. Just... tell me."

"Right," he said, giving himself a little nod. "Fragments. Images."

But he didn't speak for the longest time. I didn't want to interrupt his process, as I could see he was definitely churning *something* over in his mind.

Instead, I closed my own eyes and summoned a mental image of his youngest brother, Thoralv. He was just nineteen, and wore no beard. He had all of his hair still, but wore it short and spiky in a way that made me suspect that he was going into the modern world to find hair products.

Not that I'd ever teased him about that. He was a good kid.

Plus, I knew just how dangerous he could be with his two curved knives in his hands. I had seen him fight trolls.

I was caught up in my sketching, adding details to the boots. All the brothers wore the same high laced boots with thick soles. Patrolling called for so much walking, often in and out of bogs or through rivers and streams too wide to jump across.

Then I realized that Thorulv was watching me sketch his brother.

"He was with you at first, wasn't he?" I asked conversationally, even as I added more shading to the folds of the cloak I had drawn around him. I doubt he'd been wearing it in July, even at night, but it was just a sketch.

"It was his idea," Thorulv said. He sounded like someone talking in their sleep, the words slow and almost muffled.

"To wait on the hilltop?" I asked.

"No. To go into the woods," Thorulv said.

"Something was in the woods?" I asked, forcing myself to focus on the details of my sketched Thoralv's spiky hair.

"Alv," Thorulv said, almost choking on the syllable.

"Thoralv was in the woods?" I asked. And this time, my pencil really did pause.

"No," he said, and swallowed hard. "Alvs were in the woods. Skogealvs and haugealvs both."

I didn't dare look up at him. But I knew he wasn't joking with me. First of all, I had gone with Thorbjorn to meet a city of dwarves, so elves being real wasn't any kind of surprise.

But both kinds of elves? And so close to Villmark?

"Forest elves and barrow elves. That's what those words mean, right?"

"Skogealvs and haugealvs, yes," Thorulv said, stubbornly insisting on the Villmark words in a way that the Thors usually didn't. I had learned Villmarker Norse, of course, although I was still pretty far from being fluent in it. Mostly, people around me just naturally shifted to English. I had yet to meet a person in Villmark who couldn't speak it, and very few who ever had even a hint of an accent.

"It matters to them, what they're called," he said, as if he'd seen all those thoughts on my face.

"Of course," I said, turning to a blank page in my sketchbook. So the word "elf" was off limits. "How many alvs did you see?" I asked.

"I don't know," he said, getting frustrated again.

"That's all right," I insisted, and started sketching. Not having met an alv, I was forced to mentally summon every drawing from every book I'd ever seen about Norse alvs.

Luckily for me, that was a lot of source material. In art school and when I was trying to make a career as a book illustrator, I had done a lot of drawings pulled from Norse mythology.

"That's a skogealv, then?" Thorulv asked, watching as I drew a tall, slender figure with fine features and long, flowing robes.

"Is it?" I asked.

"Their ears are not so pointed," he said. "And they tend to wear their hair much longer."

I had drawn a woman with hair down to her waist. He watched intently as I added more locks. Then more. Then more.

He didn't seem satisfied until the woman had a train of it trailing across the ground behind her.

"Seriously?" I asked. It seemed impractical for a life deep in the woods. But he nodded.

"Do the haugealvs look the same?" I asked.

"Eh," he said noncommittally. "Their hair is usually shorter because it's curlier. And their ears *are* more pointed, like you were drawing before. But mostly the differences between the two are in their clothes."

"How so?" I asked, turning to another page and waiting with pencil tip on the paper.

He sort of half-closed his eyes as if picturing something. "Well, haugealvs wear thicker, more practical clothes in browns and dark greens. Earthy, you know? They're almost like dwarves, with their thick belts and heavy boots."

"Right," I said, trying to capture all those details in what was, to be fair, a very hasty sketch.

"Skogealvs, on the other hand, are from the forest, but also from the sky. They wear finer materials in blues and lighter greens. I don't mean finer as in nicer. Just… thinner and more flowy."

"Like an alv court," I said as I drew.

"Well, they were both alv courts in the woods," he said dismissively.

"They were?" I asked.

He opened his eyes as if he'd just heard his own words. But then he nodded solemnly. "They were. A skogealv court and a haugealv court both."

"Two courts meeting in the forest south of Villmark," I said. "Isn't that strange?"

"'Strange' isn't the word I'd use for it," Thorulv said, clenching a fist. "No, the word I'd use is more like 'problem'."

"That's what you and Thoralv were doing in the woods?" I asked. "Going to meet these two courts?"

"No, we didn't even know they were in there," he said. His face was flushed, but I couldn't tell if this was from raw emotion or from the rush of returning bits of memory.

"You were looking for the two missing patrols," I said.

"Yes, that's right!" he said, slamming his fist into his palm. "We were looking for the six missing men. But there was no sign of a fight, no sign of those maras who held us captive before. Or that woman who controlled them."

"That's what you feared it was?" I asked, not liking that idea at all. But I had been in that field. If maras had used nightmares to trap those young men like they had the Thors, I would've sensed it.

And the woman who had masterminded it all? I definitely would've sensed her.

And I would've sensed danger. Which I specifically hadn't.

"We wanted to be very sure," Thorulv said quietly.

"I don't blame you," I said. "But it wasn't maras or that woman. It was these alvs?"

"That's just it, I'm not sure," Thorulv said, frustration creeping back into his voice. "I know we went into the woods. I think it was Thoralv's idea. He suspected the patrols had been lured by something into the trees, and that's why there was no evidence of anything being done to them. Nothing else made sense, so I agreed."

"And then you found these two courts? Were they together, or did you find them separately?"

"That's just it, I don't know," he said, pressing his fingertips hard enough into his temples that his knuckles went white. "I remember Thoralv and I walking into the woods, and then I remember running back out again. Running to you. I was chanting as I ran, trying to remember what I wanted to tell you. But the minute I stopped running, I took a breath. And all those words I had been chanting just fell out of my head. I don't know."

"But you remember alvs in between those two events?"

"Just fragments of images, but I know it was from last night. It's been years since I've seen a single alv, let alone an entire tribe of them. Let alone *two* tribes of them, I mean. And Thoralv never has," he said.

"I don't know anything about alvs or their magic," I said with a sigh, looking down at my hasty drawings. "I sensed something on that hilltop, but it didn't feel evil."

"They aren't evil, no more than humans are," Thorulv agreed.

"Some humans are quite evil," I said, thinking of Halldis.

"I suppose some alvs are too," he conceded. "But they've always preferred to keep to themselves. They've never been any sort of problem before. But they've also never been this close."

"So why are they here now, and what did they do to Thoralv?" I asked.

Thorulv didn't answer. He just put his face in his hands again.

This time, I was pretty sure there were a few tears.

CHAPTER EIGHT

I GOT up from my chair as quietly as I could and went about the business of making tea for myself and the strongest coffee I could brew for Thorulv.

I had tasted their family's coffee before, the coffee they kept brewed and hot in the largest urn I had ever seen. I doubted I could match it for strength, not with the French roast beans I had on hand. But in that moment, I was pretty sure Thorulv would accept anything.

And he definitely needed me to not be lingering around and watching him for a few minutes.

I had just put a few slices of bread on the cast-iron pan on the camp stove when I realized that Mjolner wasn't there. He had been there beside me as I slept. I didn't remember any dreams, but I remembered that constant purr keeping me down in the deepest of sleeps.

But he wasn't there now. And I couldn't exactly remember if he'd been there when I had gotten up. The first few moments of the morning had been a bit of a confusing rush.

I spread a thick layer of peanut butter on the toast, divided it between two plates, and carried one of the plates plus a big mug of fresh coffee over to where Thorulv was just lowering his hands from his face again.

I ignored the wet blotchiness of his cheeks, just thrust the plate of toast into his hands.

"Eat," I said.

He nodded, but he took the coffee from my other hand first. He gulped down a large swallow, almost but didn't quite make a face, then gave me a sincere nod of thanks.

Yeah, not his home brew. But better than nothing.

I went back into my kitchen to pour out a mug of tea for myself. I had just set the kettle back on its burner when I happened to glance up and out the little window over the sink.

And saw Thorbjorn emerging from the trees to the west, my black cat stalking beside him, the pair of them looking for all the world like a hunter with his hound.

It was like Thorbjorn brought the sun with him. Which made no sense. The sun was rising on the far side of the clearing. But that reddish-gold light danced over his hair and beard. I felt warmer just watching him walk towards me.

"Your brother is here," I said to Thorulv, then quickly added, "Thorbjorn," before he got his hopes up.

"He's supposed to be in the north," Thorulv said with a studious frown.

"Sorry. I think my cat fetched him," I said.

"No, it's good he's here," Thorulv said even as I opened the door to let the two of them in.

"Ingrid," Thorbjorn said, as his face lit up at the sight of me. Like he felt warmer being near to me, too. My own heart was doing fluttering somersaults that doubled in speed at that look in his eyes.

"Thorbjorn," Thorulv said, with the definite air of announcing his presence. Thorbjorn and I might have just been standing there too long, gazing at each other.

"Thorulv," Thorbjorn said, taken aback to find his brother there.

Well, as much as Mjolner could talk to Loke in something like words, that didn't extend to Thorbjorn anymore than it did to me.

No, all the cat would've been able to convey was that he was needed.

So walking in my door at the crack of dawn to find his own oldest brother here in my tiny little cabin drinking my coffee and eating my peanut butter? Maybe it looked bad.

But even as I saw the puzzled confusion in his eyes, it quickly passed away, never quite turning to what would seem to be the obvious suspicion.

"Something's happened," he said instead.

"I'll get you some coffee while your brother explains," I said, closing the door behind him.

Mjolner crossed the room to hop up onto my bed. He turned around and around on my pillow, then curled up for a well-deserved nap.

"As if I could explain," Thorulv said bitterly.

"Well, someone needs to tell me something," Thorbjorn said good-naturedly.

"Thoralv is missing. We can start with that," Thorulv said.

"But is that something you really remember?" I asked. "Or is it possible that he, like you, found himself compelled to run away, only in some other direction? Perhaps he's down in Runde at my grand-mother's house, just for one. Or your parents."

"Compelled?" Thorbjorn asked, more concerned now.

"Was I compelled?" Thorulv asked. But himself, not me. "Yes. I was compelled to leave. I think that's true. But running, and to you, those were my choices."

"I'm missing… everything," Thorbjorn said, giving me a little nod of thanks as I put a mug of coffee in his hands. He took a sip, then set it on the table beside his chair. If the taste bothered him at all, his face didn't show it.

"Two patrols have gone missing while crossing the same hill south of Villmark," I said. "Just north of Loke's house. Loke was the one who told me about it. The council said they'd already told all of you."

"Not all of us," Thorulv corrected me. "Just Thoralv and I."

"So you went to investigate," Thorbjorn guessed. I pointed at

Thorulv's plate of toast and Thorbjorn gave me a little nod, intent on his brother. But then he looked away from Thorulv to give me a look that I couldn't describe even if I wanted to. But I knew it meant yes to toast, but two or three times that amount.

Despite the circumstances, I was almost inclined to laugh at that look. But I swallowed it down and went to put the cast-iron pan back on the camp stove.

"We were told to just sit in the grass and watch," Thorulv said.

"Sounds like a Brigida plan," Thorbjorn said neutrally.

Thorulv made a scoffing noise.

"So, what did you do instead?" Thorbjorn asked.

"We watched," Thorulv said. "For a while. Then Thoralv said he'd heard rumors. Rumors of alvs in the woods."

Thorbjorn frowned at that. "I've heard no such rumors."

"But you and Frór have been very far to the north," Thorulv said. "And for a very long time."

I turned the bread over on the rack to toast the other side, and was inwardly grateful that I wasn't the only one who thought it had been a very long time.

But all Thorbjorn said was, "Skogealvs or haugealvs?"

"Oh, that's the interesting part. Both," Thorulv said, and took another long drink of coffee.

And fought another grimace, I noticed, as I smeared peanut butter on the toast.

"Why are they here?" Thorbjorn mused.

"That I don't know," Thorulv said. "I don't remember meeting them at all. Thoralv and I walked into that forest together, and then I ran out of it. Alone. Everything in the middle is just… random fragments of things too vague to even call memories."

"No, I meant, why would both tribes be here? And together? They are not exactly known for getting along," Thorbjorn said. He was deep in thought, tugging at his lip. But that gesture was more than a little distracting. I forced myself to focus on my own tea and toast.

I had a feeling I was going to wish later that I'd made some eggs. It felt like this was the start of what was going to be a very long day. But after nine days in the woods, my icebox was pretty well tapped out.

"Hunting together? Scouting? What do you think?" Thorbjorn asked his brother.

"No, it wasn't just random hunters or warriors. It was the entire courts," Thorulv said. "I'm quite certain of that."

"The skogealv king himself is in the woods south of town?" Thorbjorn asked, alarmed.

"And the haugealv council of three, both," Thorulv said, nodding.

"Why are they here?" Thorbjorn mused again. Then he got up to pace, although in my little one-room cabin there wasn't space for more than a couple of steps in any direction.

"Maybe they're missing people as well," I said. "Maybe they are hunting the thing that took our men."

"Maybe," Thorbjorn said, but I could tell he was thinking it was something else.

Then he stopped pacing to stare down at his brother. "Something is driving them out of the wilder lands."

"Yes, I admit, I've been thinking much the same," Thorulv said. "It's possible I even thought it last night. It was Thoralv's idea to go into the woods, but I agreed for a reason I don't recall at the moment."

"Well, there's just one thing to be done about it now," Thorbjorn said with a shrug as he collapsed back down into the chair and reached for the last of his toast.

"No," Thorulv said firmly.

"It has to be us," Thorbjorn said around a mouthful of toast. I thought he meant the two of them were going to confront these Alvs.

But then he gestured towards me and himself.

"No," Thorulv said again.

"She's the volva," Thorbjorn told his brother. "Whatever happened to you, it won't happen again if she's there."

"So I go with her," Thorulv said.

"No, that's my place," Thorbjorn said.

"All three of us, then," Thorulv said.

"No, brother," Thorbjorn said, gently but firmly. "Someone needs to tell our parents what has happened."

"Right," Thorulv said. He sounded completely despondent. Like he was accepting some sentence for a crime he had pleaded guilty to.

"It's possible that he's there already, or with my grandmother," I pointed out for a second time.

"Possible," Thorulv said, not quite agreeing.

"She's not wrong," Thorbjorn told him. "You should find out for sure that no one has seen him before you worry our mother, at any rate."

"Yes, that would be wise," Thorulv said with a sigh. "You really want to go in there without any backup?"

"I'm going with him," I said.

Thorbjorn just shrugged at his brother.

"Fine. But you have the horn if you need to call the rest of us. Unless you left that with Frór?"

Thorbjorn patted the curve of the hunting horn that hung from his belt, resting against his hip.

"Very well. Hopefully, this is all just some cultural misunderstanding that can be quickly resolved," Thorulv said.

"Like the last dozen or so times we've crossed paths with the alvs," Thorbjorn agreed. Then he got up from his chair to walk his brother to the door.

"I should get dressed," I said, looking down at my pajamas. If the skogealvs really lived in a hall in the sky, they'd probably appreciate my pajamas. They were blue like the sky, and covered in fluffy white clouds.

But the haugealvs might feel like I was subtly picking sides.

"I'll wait outside," Thorbjorn said. But he hesitated before going out the door.

"What is it?" I asked.

"I need to warn you about the alvs. I mean, *do* I need to?" he asked.

"I guess I know they can be tricky," I said. Now, instead of a collection of sketches of alvs, my mental librarian was combing the same reference books for stories. "Like lawyers, only more so?"

"Not a bad analogy," Thorbjorn mused. "If lawyers are specifically trying to steer you onto the rocks while pretending to guide you to open waters."

"I think some do," I said, not quite grinning. "Hopefully not most, though."

"Ingrid," he said, and gripped both my arms almost too tightly. "They *will* try to steer you onto the rocks. They will try to trap you. And they'll use your own words to do it. Whatever happens, don't accept any agreements with them. Better yet, check with me before you accept any object or gesture from them at all. And never, ever make them a promise."

"I swear I will follow your lead in everything. And I'll be careful," I said.

He accepted this with a nod, then let me go.

"Do you think that's what happened to Thoralv and the patrols? They made an agreement or a promise?" I asked.

"I don't know," Thorbjorn said as he opened the door to step out into the morning air.

But then he looked back at me with a grin. "Get dressed so we can go find out."

CHAPTER NINE

IT WAS a pleasant morning for a walk through the woods, although the warmth of the air was hinting that it would get stifling before the afternoon. Our reprieve from July humidity was sadly over.

I was wearing what I thought of as my volva uniform, the long dress in alternating red and green panels with white sleeves so voluminous I had to work to keep them from dragging on the ground or catching on the branches of the trees around us.

My bronze wand was tucked into a loop in my belt. I hoped I wouldn't need it for actual magic, as I wasn't particularly skilled with it. But even just on its own, it was a powerful symbol. If I was going to dress to impress, I couldn't leave it at home.

My grandmother's grandmother's gold cat brooch completed the outfit. And the black cat walking beside me completed the whole look. I was as prepared to meet a royal court as I'd ever be.

Which didn't feel so very prepared.

Thorbjorn had changed his tunic to the spare he carried in his pack, but it was little cleaner than the one he had been wearing when he walked up to my cabin. And there wasn't much he could do about the weeks' worth of mud that flecked his boots. Or the fact that his hair and beard both could use a tidying trim.

But even disheveled as he was, he still had a lordly air to him. It was just part of how he stood and how he walked. He wasn't a man to be trifled with.

Plus, he'd dealt with these alvs before. I had no doubt they knew his worth as well as I did.

We had skirted the village proper, sticking to the woods west of town. Neither of us said so out loud, but I think we were of a mind.

We wanted every minute we could get of the two of us alone.

Well, alone with Mjolner.

Which, as always, couldn't be leisurely minutes. Because of our responsibilities. But we took what we could get.

I told Thorbjorn all I had been up to while he had been away, and he told me the things he and Frór had seen to the north. Mostly trolls, beings I had seen before. But Thorbjorn is a born storyteller. He had me laughing even as we drew closer to our destination.

And the laughter kept me from getting too nervous.

At least, until I saw the first of the silken tents through the trees. We were approaching a glade completely enclosed by trees, in a hollow nestled amongst taller hills. I guessed I was looking at skogealv tents and pavilions, as they favored blues and light greens like the first grass of spring. But beyond them, on the far side of the grassy meadow, I could just discern dome-shaped tents of browns and dark greens that nearly blended with the grass and trees around them.

That must be the haugealv camp.

Thorbjorn caught my elbow and guided me to circle the skogealv tents while still well back amongst the trees. Only when we reached the open space between the two camps did we turn to enter the glade, into that no-man's-land between.

Someone had spotted us as we approached. Not that we'd been trying to sneak up or anything. But as we stepped into the bright morning sun in the center of the glade, alvs from both camps stood silently watching us, waiting to see what we would do.

The weather had definitely made a turn to a more typical hot and humid July. We had been walking in the shade, but that walk had taken more than an hour. And I was, admittedly, overdressed. The dress was made from linen, not wool, but it was long-sleeved and the skirt was so full it hung around me in overlapping folds.

I was sweaty, which was uncomfortable. But I also had the beginnings of a dehydration headache, which went beyond uncomfortable to an actual impediment. My mind felt fuzzy, like I couldn't quite think as nimbly as usual. Even my vision was getting a little foggy, especially as we approached the treeless center of the glade.

I made a mental note to bring water the next time we went on an expedition together. Then I made another note, this time of the irony of expecting to remember anything I made a mental note of while in a state of brain fog.

But I blinked a few times to bring my vision into something like focus, swallowed to clear some of the dryness from my throat, and forced my mind to just power through the fog.

It was time to make a plan.

"Which camp do we go to first?" I whispered to Thorbjorn.

Before he could answer me, a woman's melodious voice carried across the glade. "Thorbjorn Valkisson. Well met. My father awaits your presence. Yours and your volva's, of course."

I turned to see a woman standing just at the edge of the skogealv camp. She was a few inches taller than me, with dark red hair that fell down her back to trail behind her. But the train of her green gown was longer still, so not a strand of that hair touched the actual ground. Her eyes were the same intense emerald as her gown, and her ears came to the subtlest of points, just poking out of her hair.

Each individual element of her appearance spoke of beauty, but all together she struck me as too cold to be really beautiful. And there was something in her eyes I just didn't like.

Especially since those eyes were fixed almost greedily on Thorbjorn.

"The king was expecting me?" Thorbjorn asked her mildly.

"Indeed, he was," she said, and gestured towards the central pavilion of white and sky blue silk panels, the largest of the tents in the glade. The panels were stirring and snapping in the breeze, but never blowing far enough apart for me to see inside.

"Then we shall speak to him first," Thorbjorn said, and took my elbow again. The woman noticed this gesture, her eyes growing colder still as she stared at his hand on my arm, but she said nothing. She merely fell into step behind us as we approached the parting in the silk panels.

Two alv men beside the tent pulled back those panels to let us pass inside. There were four more men inside, all dressed alike. The swords at their sides made the sameness of their indigo pants and cerulean tunics feel like military uniforms. But not even a dress uniform would look so fine, the silk of their tunics so sheer it, too, danced in the breeze.

These six men were more than dressed alike, they were all similar in appearance as well. Their fine blond hair was worn to the same waist-length, and the top was arranged in the same neat half knot. Their eyes varied from blue to green, but not a lot.

They didn't quite look like brothers, though. Maybe cousins, although I didn't think that was quite the case either.

Honestly, it struck me as if someone were recruiting for a slightly older than usual boy band, and had put out a casting call for a very specific sort of look. And these six young men had been the top picks.

At the moment, they were arranged along the sides of a long, white carpet that led from the tent opening to a raised dais on the far side of the pavilion. And on that dais was a simple three-legged stool, much like the ones the high council in Villmark sat on.

But the man perched on this stool was very different from anyone on our high council. He wore an outfit of so many overlapping layers, all in shades of blue and green patterned silks, it reminded me of the junihitoe of Heian Era Japanese women. Someone else must have helped arrange the folds, as they fell so artfully around him as he sat on that stool, his hands folded formally on his lap.

He had the same dark red hair as the woman who had led us to this tent, but there was something ageless about his face. The skin was as soft as a youth's, but there was something ancient in his green eyes. He wasn't as cold as that woman, but that was only a matter of degrees.

I mean, I doubted *anyone* could be colder than she was.

Even as I thought this, she swept past me in a rustle of silk, gliding up the steps, then taking a place just behind and to the right side of the man on the stool.

Thorbjorn inclined his head ever so slightly in acknowledgment as he said, "King Alarik. Princess Lianna. It has been seven years since I saw you last, and that was very far from this glade. We are well met, I hope?"

"I think you know we are not," King Alarik said. "Why else would we have summoned you?"

"I didn't realize I had been summoned specifically," Thorbjorn said. "Was it you who sent the cat?"

King Alarik looked briefly confused. Then he noticed Mjolner sitting on the ground just to my left, washing his ears.

"That's not a cat," he said at last. But there was just a hint of a question in his words.

Thorbjorn shrugged in a way that conveyed not so much as a lack of knowledge of the answer, but a lack of interest in the question.

But then again, even I didn't know what Mjolner was, really.

"We sent your brother," the princess Lianna said.

"I see. Did you send him to fetch me before or after you played with his memory?"

Thorbjorn spoke with a jocular tone, but I didn't think any of us in that tent were fooled. He was deadly serious. And although he made no change in his posture, standing casually with his hand still on my arm, I noticed two of the alv men around us put their hands on the hilts of their swords.

The king gave the two of them an icy stare, then turned his attention back to Thorbjorn. "That is a serious accusation."

"Yes. It is," Thorbjorn said.

"I saw him on his way myself," Lianna said. "He was quite lucid when he left me, I promise you."

"You promise me," Thorbjorn said musingly. But she just arched an eyebrow at him.

Clearly they were having some private nonverbal exchange I

wasn't understanding. But what did it mean, that she promised Thorulv was lucid when he left her? That she hadn't done anything?

Or that whatever she had done, it hadn't taken effect right away?

I longed to rub at my aching temples. Not that I thought it would help to clear my mind. It was so very hard to think inside that stuffy tent. But I would bet on the latter scenario.

But I couldn't be sure.

"I take it your brother found his way to you in the end, even if he appears to have lost the message on the way," King Alarik said.

"That seems to have been the case," Thorbjorn said. "But you say you summoned me, and I'm here now. I would ask you how I may be of service, but I'm afraid that has to be the second thing we discuss."

"Yes, there is the matter of your other brother," the king agreed.

"So you know where he is?" I asked. The king's eyes turned to fix on me for the first time, and I felt like a cold wind had suddenly danced up my spine. The hair on the back of my neck was instantly on end.

But this wasn't a useful blast of cold. It wasn't like rolling down the window when driving late at night, when the chill wind would wake my mind back up and I could focus on the driving again. No, this was just an energy-sapping cold.

I found myself tracing a bind rune in the air, just a quick invocation of Fe, Thurs and Kaun because they all spoke of warmth to me. It was a subtle motion, just one finger moving even as my arms stayed straight by my sides.

But I was pretty sure Alarik noticed what I was doing. He didn't react, but it was almost like I could sense him smirking on the inside.

"Indeed," the king said at last, blinking slowly much like Mjolner did—only with both eyes—before turning his gaze back on Thorbjorn. "The haugealvs have him. As agreed."

"Who agreed?" I asked.

But I could feel Thorbjorn beside me bristling, every muscle tensing up. Like he knew the answer already.

And he didn't like it.

"Tell me," he said to the king, his voice a low growl. More hands reached for hilts, but this time the king didn't shoot anyone any chastising looks.

"Your youngest brother stands accused of murder," Lianna said. "He refused to confess. But he agreed to surrender to our—meaning both tribes of alvs'—authority. The haugealvs are holding him until sunset tomorrow, per the terms of his own oath. He promised that the two of you would find the real killer and clear his name, but if you do not, Thoralv Valkisson has already agreed to be put to death in the killer's place."

"Killer?" I repeated. Although every word she had just uttered was sticking in my mind.

What had Thoralv done? And why?

I didn't think even for a minute that he'd killed anyone in cold blood. Or even in the heat of battle, not if it was someone like an alv that was meant to be an ally. None of the brothers were that casual with violence.

So why did he surrender the way he did? He hadn't confessed, so he wasn't pleading that it was a justifiable death under Viking era norms, where killing was sometimes allowable but covering up the killing was not.

He should've walked away with Thorulv and gone back to Villmark. If the alvs had proof of his guilt, they should have brought it before the Villmark high council and pleaded their case.

So why had he surrendered? It made no sense to me.

Unless he'd somehow been tricked into it? Thorbjorn had warned me that alvs were tricky. Was this proof of that?

I didn't have any doubt the two of us could find a killer. We'd done exactly that many times before. But there was no reason to threaten Thorbjorn's brother to make us investigate. If there was truly a killer on the loose, then we were already prepared to do the job. No one needed any leverage to force us to do so.

So why had the alvs insisted on holding him hostage?

"I must speak with him," Thorbjorn said darkly.

"That is not up to me," the king said, raising his hands as if to show how empty they were of the power to grant that wish.

"Then we shall speak with the haugealvs," Thorbjorn said, and I felt his hand on my arm tighten, like he was about to turn us both around to go.

But I said, "Wait. I need someone to tell me exactly what is going on here. Who was killed, precisely?"

"Tolkki," Lianna said, her eyes on Thorbjorn. From the look on his face, I gathered he had known this person, and this news came as a shock. But not of grief. More of surprise.

"My finest warrior," the king said to me. "The man destined to be my daughter's betrothed. Brutally murdered and cruelly left in her path, for her to find. The haugealvs find it convenient to accuse your brother, but the evidence is scant. And, given the nature of our negotiations, it is hard not to see how they benefit from putting me off balance. Although using my daughter to do it is very low of them."

The coldness of his demeanor heated up with those words, and one of his neatly folded hands shifted position into a tight fist.

"What negotiations?" Thorbjorn asked, that dangerous edge back in his voice.

That wasn't my first question, but now that it had been spoken, I was curious to hear the answer.

"That is an alv matter," the king said with an edge of his own.

"We can't solve the crime without knowing all the details," I said.

"You will be supplied with all relevant details," the king said.

I felt like I'd just been dismissed from his mind. And yet I was still standing there.

"They will all be relevant," Thorbjorn said. But he was looking at me, not at the king or his daughter. "I don't need to speak with Thoralv to know why he gave himself up as a hostage. He was trying to prevent further bloodshed. These men around us were all prepared to take a haugealv life for the skogealv life lost."

"You say the proof against Thoralv is scant. But is there any proof that a haugealv was behind the murder?" I asked. I had been looking up at Thorbjorn as he spoke to me, but I started to shift my eyes over to the king. He seemed the most likely person to have the answer to that question.

But Thorbjorn gave me a quick shake of his head, then an imploring look.

He needed to have a conversation with me, but not one we could have in the middle of that tent. But until I knew what he was thinking, it wasn't safe for me to press the matter.

He could convey a lot with those eyes of his, I swear. My head ached too hard for me to think clearly, but understanding his looks always came so easily to me.

I gave in with a nod.

"Come, Ingrid Torfudottir," Thorbjorn said, gripping my arm again.

"But I still have so many more questions," I said even as I let him draw me away, Mjolner close at my heels.

"I know," he said softly to me. But then he looked up at the king. "We'll be back."

"I'll be here," the king said. "Ready when you return to help you tease apart all the haugealv lies you are about to hear."

Thorbjorn just gave him a curt nod. Then the two of us swept back out of the tent.

I didn't have to turn my head to know that Lianna was still glaring at Thorbjorn's hand on my arm as we left. I could feel that gaze like the burn of cold metal on my skin.

The intense heat from the July sun was almost a welcome relief from all that ice.

CHAPTER TEN

It wasn't terribly surprising to find a pair of haugealvs waiting for us when we emerged from the skogealv camp to cross the open grass in the center of the glade. They didn't come out to meet us, and it occurred to me that both camps were avoiding stepping out into the open space between them. The tense feeling of being watched was, if anything, even stronger than before.

But these two waiting for us were not soldiers, and neither looked like a princess. They both wore pants of soft, dark brown leather and tunics in different shades of piney green. Well made, but not so fine as what the skogealv royalty had worn, and definitely not meant to be any kind of military uniform.

Although I was beginning to see that age was a hard thing to gauge in alvs. The man and the woman watching us approach looked to be somewhere between middle age and late middle age. Neither had so much as a hint of sliver or gray to their hair, and their faces showed only the finest of lines, but they had a gravitas about them that spoke of a life measured in long decades.

They both had hair of a rich auburn, appearing brown in the shadows of the round tents of their camp, but catching the sunlight in streaks of reddish gold as they stepped forward to greet us. The man's was longer, tucked behind his pointed ears to fall in a straight curtain down his back. The woman's was braided in a hundred fine braids, then those braids were braided together into thicker plaits, and those plaits were twisted around in an elaborate pattern that didn't extend past the high collar of her tunic, but that made it impossible to guess just how long it would all be if she took it down.

"Well met, Fedder," Thorbjorn said to the man, and offered his hand in greeting. The haugealv man grasped Thorbjorn's forearm in both of his hands and gave him something between a handshake and a hug.

"Well met, young Valkisson," the man said. "With me is the newest member of our high council, Rajka."

The woman gave first Thorbjorn and then me a formal nod.

"I am Thorbjorn, third of the Valkissons, and this is one of the volvas of Villmark, Ingrid Torfudottir," Thorbjorn said.

"My apologies for not recalling your name. I find humans in general hard to tell apart, and you and your brothers particularly so," Fedder said. "I hope you will not take offense."

"Not on that account," Thorbjorn said somewhat ominously. "We have much to discuss. But where is your third?"

The woman, Rajka, spoke. "Valeria awaits us by the central fire in our camp. She is old, even by our measure of such things, and does not stray far from the warmth of the flames. Even on days as hot as this one is shaping into."

We followed the two of them through the haugealv camp. Where the skogealv tents had been neatly arranged in rows and columns, with all the tent openings lined up like so many front doors in a suburban development, the haugealv camp was far more random. The round tents clustered tightly together in some places, but were further apart in others. Even the tent pegs had been driven into the ground with no apparent rhyme or reason, and I had to take care not to trip over the many lines that held the tents in place.

Then we broke out of the clusters of tents into another opening under the blue sky. There were others gathered around the remains of a bonfire, but when Rajka called out a few words I didn't understand, most of them faded away into the tents around us.

But not all of them. Like in the skogealv camp, six young, armed men were standing around us, although not in uniform and not in any particular formation.

But unlike in the skogealv camp, there were also six young, armed women standing amongst them.

Neither group was giving me the same casting call for a vocal band vibes. The clothes indeed stuck to a range between browns and dark greens, but they sported a variety of hairstyles and simple jewelry, and their eyes were in every shade imaginable.

I followed Thorbjorn to the far side of the bonfire, where a woman both incredibly old and and incredibly tiny was huddled under a few layers of blankets in something that was halfway between a chair and a basket. She could sit in it, but it would be no trouble for two or four of the young people around her to pick that seat up by the woven loops that adorned its back and sides and carry her to wherever she needed to go.

Unlike the other alvs, her face was deeply lined. She looked like one of those dolls whose heads are made from shriveled crab-apples. The hands that were folded on top of those blankets were like bird talons, little more than bones curled into themselves.

But her blue eyes when she looked up at us were sharp and intelligent, and her voice when she spoke was unwavering and filled the camp clearing like the sonorous tone of a bell.

"Well met, Valkisson and volva," she said. "We have much to discuss with you."

"First, I must ask to be allowed to see my brother," Thorbjorn said.

"You may not," Valeria said, but with genuine regret in her voice and eyes. "He dictated the terms of his surrender to us, and it is not within our power to alter them."

"To be clear," Fedder said, "your brother surrendered to both camps. It is not within the power of our camp alone to alter those terms, even though he has been placed in our charge."

"And we do not think coming to an agreement on that matter with

King Alarik will end any more happily than the many other things we've come here to negotiate with him," Rajka added. "He is most obstinate. And the loss of his man has only made him more so."

"The king didn't seem to think my brother was guilty of this crime," Thorbjorn said.

The three haugealv council members exchanged too many communicative glances to really be considered polite. I suspected they were silently debating how much to say to Thorbjorn and me.

At last, it was the oldest of them who spoke.

"Both tribes have agreed that you shall be the final arbiter of justice in this manner. It is not surprising King Alarik has already started wooing you to his side," Valeria said, wrinkling her nose in a show of disdain. But she gave in with a shrug. "But in fairness, we don't find the evidence against Thoralv compelling, either. It's just that nothing points to anyone else. And someone needed to stand up and be tried."

I chewed at my lip, irritated by this response, but mostly because I knew I was out of my depth. I was still working to understand how the Villmarkers saw such things as justice and courts, and crime and punishment. Apparently the alv versions of all those things were another flavor entirely.

It sounded so insane, arresting someone almost at random just because *someone* had to be arrested. What if there hadn't been a volunteer?

I had to trust that it all made sense to them. Their culture was older than I knew. They must have found a way of finding justice that worked for them.

But it was all so opaque to me.

And I had no time to learn any of it except on the fly.

"I don't suppose it would do any good to ask if you know who killed this Tolkki fellow?" I asked.

"If we knew, so many things that have happened since could've been averted," Fedder said.

"It nearly came to real bloodshed," Valeria said. "Your brother interceded. We well know the thanks we owe him for that. We have no desire to see him executed as a proxy. And we will assist your investigation in any way we can."

"That will be appreciated," I said.

But Fedder was already shaking his head sadly. "We will help, of course, but there is very little help we can offer. The man was killed well beyond the borders of our camp, in fact on the far side of the skogealv camp. Not a one of us saw anything suspicious before, during, or after the murder must have occurred."

"Which is why we so readily agreed to your brother's offer of himself as a hostage to justice," Rajka said. "There is little we can do to solve this. And there seems to be little the skogealv king is willing to do. Thoralv offered us our only solution."

"Save returning to the wilds of the north," Fedder said, with the air of someone stating something they've said many times before.

"Which we cannot do," Valeria said, again like she was rehashing something *she* had said in response each time.

Rajka just sighed.

"You can see why your involvement is so necessary," Fedder said almost apologetically. "I realize that you can't be impartial since you're not uninvolved, as it is your brother who stands accused. But murder is more common among humans than it is among alvs. We have no experience in investigating such things. But you two do."

Thorbjorn just nodded. Then he shot me a quick look, but one I understood at once.

We shared a desire to argue about the commonality of murder in Villmark, but that desire was thwarted by the awkward fact that murders just kept happening.

"I have a question you can probably answer," I said instead. "There are six men and six women in this clearing with us who didn't leave when you dismissed the others. They're all armed, and yet they don't strike me as being an honor guard or anything like that."

"No, they are allowed to stay because this matter involves them most of all," Rajka said. "They volunteered for the bridal tribute, before the skogealvs refused to make the exchange."

"That happened before the body was found," Fedder said to me. He shot Rajka a sharp look, but then looked back to me again. "We are not in agreement on that being a related matter."

"Can we back up a bit?" I asked. "What's a bridal tribute?"

"An exchange of brides for the purpose of sealing the terms of a negotiation," Thorbjorn told me, and Fedder nodded his agreement with that statement.

"The six haugealv women with us had volunteered to go with the skogealv camp when our two tribes parted ways. To marry six of their men and live among them for as long as both saw fit. And the men here were meant to be the grooms, receiving the six skogealv brides," Rajka said.

"The wedding was canceled because of the murder?" I said. Then corrected myself, "No, you said the wedding was canceled first, and then the body was found?"

"Not *canceled*," Valeria said.

"Well," Fedder said, and for a moment I thought the two of them were going to resume some old argument. But then he turned to me instead. "We had negotiated everything with the skogealv king. Everything had been agreed to. All that remained was for our six brides to go over to their camp, and for their six brides to come over to ours. Then the weddings would've taken place. Only after that was done would the formal agreement between our two tribes be signed, and then we'd all go our separate ways."

"What happened instead of all that?" I asked.

"Yesterday, at the appointed time, when the sun was highest in the sky, our six brides started to cross the glade to where their grooms were waiting in the skogealv camp," Fedder said. "And our six grooms were standing ready at the edge of our camp to meet their own brides."

"But the skogealv brides didn't come," Thorbjorn guessed.

"Was that princess one of the brides?" I asked.

"No, she was not," Valeria said with a twist of annoyance to her mouth. "She is, as you said, a princess. But we aren't ruled by a king. We have no prince for her to marry. No, the six brides meant to live among us were six ordinary skogealv women."

"Although perhaps not volunteers," Rajka put in.

"We don't know that for a fact," Fedder said to her.

"And yet they refused to come at the appointed time," Rajka said. "Perhaps they changed their minds, but I find it far more likely they had never been willing in the first place."

"The skogealv grooms were all the king's personal guards, under the command of Tolkki before he died," Fedder told us.

"Which is why we're not sure any of the volunteers from their tribe were proper volunteers," Rajka said. "The skogealvs do things differently than we do in many ways."

"The absence of the skogealv brides caused all of your negotiations to fall apart," Thorbjorn guessed.

"Yes. At first we hoped it would only be a temporary setback," Fedder said. "When the skogealv women didn't appear, King Alarik seemed as taken by surprise as any of the three of us."

"But *then* the body was found," Valeria said. "And then the accusations started."

"And everything really did fall apart," Fedder said.

"And my brother stepped in at that point?" Thorbjorn asked.

"Your two brothers came into the camp just as swords were being drawn," Rajka said. "They tried first to offer to be a neutral third party in further negotiations, but it was simply too late for that. And then someone—and for the life of me, I don't know who or from which camp—someone accused your brother of the killing. There was no blood to be seen on his blades when he showed them to us, but the two of them did emerge from the woods near where the body had been found."

"Perfectly understandably; that is the direction where the easiest path to Villmark lies," Fedder put in.

"It scarcely matters," Rajka said, fisting her hands in frustration. "With that young skogealv warrior dead, there was no going back to the table for King Alarik, even if your brother had confessed and ended the matter then and there."

"It was all falling apart. The skogealvs were going to pack up and leave. And that would've led to war. That's when your brother swore his vows and made himself our hostage," Fedder said. "We don't like to take such vows. Not from humans. We consider you our kin."

"As we consider you our ancestors," Thorbjorn said with a little bow of his head. "But there was no need to hold him in order to bring me here. If you had asked, I would've come."

"We both would've come," I said. "A man has been murdered, and the guilty party must be found. We don't have to be coerced into helping with that."

"We took his oath when he offered it only because it was necessary before King Alarik would agree," Fedder said. "Without your brother putting himself up as hostage in place of the unknown guilty party, there was no way to stop the king from trying to slaughter us all."

"That seems extreme," I grumbled. Thorbjorn shot me a sympathetic look. Which was weird. It was his brother's life on the line. Why was he taking it so much more calmly than I was?

"We will find the guilty party," Thorbjorn said to the haugealv council. "You have our word."

"By sunset tomorrow," Valeria said.

Those words finally got a reaction out of Thorbjorn. I could feel him bristling as he stood beside me, and his brow was furrowing in the beginnings of real anger.

"Your brother's terms," Fedder said.

"Well," Rajka interjected, despite Fedder's glower. "Thoralv swore of his own free will, of course. But what he swore was only what he had to for the king to hear him at all. None of you Valkissons are fools, not even the youngest among you."

"So we have a deadline," Thorbjorn said in a low growl. "It won't matter. We were already prepared to start at once."

Then he took my hand in his and pulled me away from the haugealv camp. But not back towards the clearing. No, he was tugging me further west, into the trees beyond the glade.

I let him pull me along, trying to find the words I could say that would help him get over his anger. We would need colder blood to solve this crime, after all.

It was only when he stopped our aggressively fast march out of camp, when all the tents behind us were lost from view behind the trees in their thick summer greenery, that I realized it wasn't anger at all that was driving him.

No, when he stopped moving, the only emotion I felt coming from him was fear and worry for his brother. He wasn't crying, but he was shaking. And when I turned to him, he collapsed against me, holding onto me with his sweaty brow pressed against the side of my neck.

I just held him until he had command of himself again. It didn't take long. Then he straightened up, dragging a sleeve across his sweat-damped face.

"The body was found over that way," he said with a vague wave of his hand back towards the south end of the skogealv camp.

"Are you ready for this?" I asked him.

"I have to be," he said.

And once more, we were speeding our way through the woods.

I couldn't think of a single murder I had solved in such a short time. But, like Thorbjorn had said, we had to.

We just had to.

CHAPTER ELEVEN

THORBJORN and I went back to the open, grassy field between the two camps in the glade, very aware that our every move was being watched. All twelve of the haugealv prospective brides and grooms were standing in twos and threes between their dome-like tents, whispering together but never taking their eyes off of the two of us, or their hands off of their weapons.

On the other side of the glade, only the six young men from the king's tent were in view. There was no sign of the king himself or his daughter.

I was grateful at least for the latter absence. But the watchful feeling was making me anxious. Everyone around us, in sight or not, was adding to a general tenseness of the atmosphere. Like everyone was waiting for the fight that Thorbjorn's brother had averted the night before to come to the fore once more.

And they expected that to happen soon.

I already had a river of sweat running down my back just from the heat of the day. I didn't need anxiety sweat on top of it.

And my headache was not easing even a little bit. Trying to think through the brain fog was too much like trying to run in waist-deep water.

"Will you draw the murder scene?" Thorbjorn asked. We were standing in the very center of the glade, and while there were signs that the grass here had been trod on by a lot of feet, and I could see the indentations where a king's stool had been set opposite three stools for a high council, there was no hint of a fight having taken place there.

"The body was found in the woods, wasn't it?" I asked him as we both scanned the grass around us for clues.

"To the south end of the camp," Thorbjorn said.

"That's really where I should start, then. Where the body was found," I said.

Thorbjorn scanned the tree line beyond the light-colored silk tents, but there were no hints of where to start.

So he crossed to the edge of the skogealv camp, to the nearest of the young men watching us. He watched Thorbjorn approach with his arms crossed, making no move towards his weapon.

"Well met," Thorbjorn said. I suspected the greeting was as much in the way of finding out whether this fellow understood Villmarker Norse or not, but the nod the man gave in answer wasn't exactly illuminating on that score.

"We weren't introduced before," I said as I too approached him. I extended a hand. "I'm sure you know I'm the volva, Ingrid Torfudottir. But I didn't get your name?"

He looked at my outstretched hand for a moment, but not so long that it got awkward. He took it in his in a brief squeeze. "I am Ilmar. My companions are Edel, Olai, Uki, Caro and Kallu."

That was how I discovered the other five had closed in around us. But I doubted they had sneaked up on Thorbjorn. He just nodded to each of them in turn.

I hoped he would be better at remembering who was who than I was doomed to be. I had caught all the names, but the faces were already blending together. I could probably repeat them in order now, but once these men started moving around, I was going to be lost.

It was just so hard to think. And it got harder the higher the sun got in the sky.

"You six were meant to be getting married today, I take it?" Thorbjorn said.

"That had been the agreement," the one I was pretty sure was Caro said. "For our part, we are still willing." He looked to the others, four of whom nodded their agreement.

"Provided you find that Tolkki died by something besides a haugealv blade," Ilmar said. But even he didn't sound like he thought that conclusion too likely.

"How were you going to sort yourselves?" I asked. "I mean, which bride was going to be matched with which groom? Were you going to get to choose? Or don't you care?"

"Our two tribes have been eating and drinking together since we arrived at this glade. And we met the haugealv brides formally yesterday," Caro said. "Only a brief meeting, but I think we were all in agreement about the matches."

"As were they?" I asked.

The one named Kallu chuckled, and then two of the others joined in. "They were the ones who did the picking and choosing," he told me.

"We just had no cause to argue," Ilmar said. "For our part, we were completely content with our intendeds."

"I hope we can solve this quickly and amicably, then," I said. "So you can get on with your happy day."

"We need to see the spot where the body was found, if you can show it to us," Thorbjorn said.

Ilmar nodded, then motioned for us to follow him, first to the south end of the skogealv camp, and then to the tree line beyond. There was a clump of squat evergreen trees here among the birches and elms, thick enough to block the view into the forest from the glade.

"The princess found him just around this stand of trees, out of sight from where the rest of us were gathered in the center of the glade," Ilmar said, ducking under a few heavy branches. On the far side, he stayed awkwardly bent under yet another branch, but pointed to the clearer ground in front of him.

Thorbjorn ducked even more awkwardly under the tree on the other side to leave me an open path into the tiny clearing ringed by evergreen trees. No grass grew here, but the ground was covered by a thick blanket of fallen needles.

That blanket had been disturbed recently. It wasn't hard to see the outline of the body, and the place where the dry ground had soaked up the blood from his wounds. Whoever had picked him up and carried him away had swept a lot of the other needles around, but that wouldn't be a problem.

For how I inspected crime scenes, such little disturbances didn't really matter.

"Thank you, Ilmar," Thorbjorn said. "Ingrid and I would like a moment alone here, if you would allow it."

"Of course," Ilmar said, and sketched a little bow at the two of us. Then he ducked back out the way we'd come, quickly vanishing from sight through the evergreen branches.

"I wonder what this Tolkki fellow was even doing in here?" I said as I unslung my art bag from across my shoulder and settled on a cleanish patch of ground.

"A perfectly useless place to stand guard," Thorbjorn said as he scanned what little we could see around us. The forest and glade both were lost to view. Our entire world was the overlapping branches of six squat but wide evergreens. "So, was he meeting someone in here, or was he lured in?"

"Hopefully, I'll have some answers in a minute," I said, turning my sketchbook to a blank page and fetching out my charcoal pencils.

But I stopped with my pencil poised, not quite making a mark on the page. "Thorbjorn, I know we came here to find Thoralv, but there are six other men who are still missing."

"I know," he said. Then he sat down on the ground beside me. Mjolner immediately climbed into his lap, but he just scratched absentmindedly at the cat's ears.

"Six missing men, two sets of six grooms and two sets of six brides," I said.

"I've noticed that as well," he said. "Maybe it's related. Or maybe it's a coincidence. Maybe someone has been killing our young men, and moved on to killing skogealv men. Or maybe Tolkki was killed because he knew something."

"Or maybe he was the killer, but now he's been stopped?" I said.

"If that were true, why would the person who did it not come forward? It would be justifiable," he said.

"Right," I said grimly. "Do the alvs follow the old Viking ways in that matter? I mean, this was a pretty important thing they were trying to accomplish. Whatever it actually is, since they won't give us even a hint. Doesn't that make killing Tolkki a crime? Because it certainly seemed to derail everything."

"It is troubling that no one stepped forward," he said. "Someone wanted to hide this. That is inherently suspicious."

"I'll see what I can learn here, but when we speak to the king and the council again, we have to ask about the other men," I said.

"Of course," Thorbjorn said. "I didn't mean to lose sight of that. It's just baffling to me, the position Thoralv got himself into. As a Valkisson, he knows better than to think he can barter with his life with alvs. And yet he did so. My mind won't rest until I know why."

"Perhaps he felt it was necessary, for the sake of the missing men?" I said.

"Perhaps," Thorbjorn said. But not in the tone I was hoping to hear.

"You don't think so," I said.

"It is probably a factor," he allowed. "But I just feel like something else is going on. Something I'm not seeing."

"The sooner we solve this, the sooner they will let him free and then we can just ask him," I said. "But in the meantime, I think we can take heart in Fedder's words. He said Thoralv was no fool. He can't explain it to us, but he clearly thinks your brother did the right thing."

Thorbjorn stewed on this for a moment, scratching all around Mjolner's ears. Then he just nodded at me. "Draw," he said, gesturing to my sketchbook. "Mjolner and I will watch over you."

A thing which was all too necessary, sadly. Because once I started drawing, I lost all awareness of the world around me.

And this time was no exception to that rule. As soon as I started moving that pencil over the paper, I lost all awareness of the piney, coppery smell of the air in that close space, of the growing heat as the sun slid ever higher into the sky.

Even of Thorbjorn, sitting so close beside me that our knees were touching.

All I knew were the images that flowed through me, faster than I could commit them to paper. I hashed them out in the crudest of sketches, drawing in thick, dark lines, filling page after page in a flurry of motion.

When I finally came out of it, the sun was almost directly overhead. I was also a little hungry. And a lot thirsty.

Way too thirsty. My headache seemed to almost be darkening my vision. The brain fog was so intense it was like I didn't actually physically exist in the world, but floated in some adjacent plane.

But I pushed all those feelings aside for the moment, turning my attention to my sketches. Thorbjorn leaned close to look over my shoulder as I turned the pages.

I had sketched Lianna finding Tolkki's body facedown just where the blood stained the ground. But this wasn't new information. We already knew she was the one who had found the body.

Although what the king had claimed, that he had been left in her path deliberately, felt completely false now that we were sitting there. This place was not exactly inaccessible, but it was inconvenient. This would never be where she was walking, not in a predictable way.

But as I turned the pages, I realized everything else I had drawn was the same curved knife. Over and over, from ten different angles, the same curved knife.

Thoralv fought with two curved knives. They were his signature weapons. But I had never gotten a close look at them. Still, I felt a growing lump in my throat.

This investigation was already taking a dark turn. And I didn't want to follow it.

But I had to.

"Do you recognize it?" I asked Thorbjorn half-heartedly. "There are some distinctive features. Something runic on the side of the blade here, but the letters aren't clear. Do they mean anything to you?"

He took the book from me to give each drawing what I was pretty sure was more attention than it deserved. Especially as, in the end, he just shook his head.

"It is not my brother's, if that is what's worrying you," he said.

"That *was* my worst fear," I admitted. Although my sense of relief at his words was strangely muted. Something was still bothering me about it.

"It must be important to have demanded your attention in this way," he said. "You drew it so many times."

He had a lot more confidence in my skills than I did.

"Maybe someone in the camp recognizes it," I said.

But after I tucked the book back in my art bag, I didn't turn back towards the glade. Rather, I parted the branches on the far side of the clearing among the trees, trying to see what lay beyond this wall of green.

"Your drawing didn't show anyone coming into or leaving this place," Thorbjorn said. "Do you think they came from that way?"

"I think I want to see to be sure," I said. "We can go see the king afterward, or ask those skogealv grooms if they recognize the knife. But since we're already in the woods, let's see what there is just a bit deeper."

Thorbjorn nodded, but gently moved me aside to take the lead.

I was about to tease him for thinking anything dangerous could be so close to the camps, when we emerged from the far side of the stand of trees to see seven tall shadows towering over us.

And despite the July sun beating down on us, I was suddenly profoundly cold.

But also, that dehydration headache and brain fog intensified, stronger than ever.

We had visited two camps, one a royal visit and the other merely a high political power one. But still, no one had offered us any water?

I rubbed at my head, but that only made it worse. And it was weird how the cold feeling from those shadows didn't help.

No, this cold was making me feel hypothermic. I had the strong impulse to lie down and sleep.

And it was scary how hard it was to remain standing, to look up, and to confront whatever was looming over us.

CHAPTER TWELVE

THAT COLD WASN'T my nervousness taking physical form.

It wasn't anything natural at all.

But it was definitely real. And it was emanating from the central of the seven shadows circling us atop a low ridge of earth under the interwoven branches of the elms overhead.

I had my bronze wand in my hand before I had even formed a thought. The six flanking shadows recoiled a bit, but the main one stood strong.

I didn't know any runes for sunlight yet, and fire felt like maybe overkill. But I could use Thurs to summon a little wind. Still thinking of that tornado, I didn't do much, just enough to stir the branches that separated us from the actual sun. We were still all in shadow, but it was a dappled shadow, not so dense as before.

My headache persisted, and I really wished I had some water. But I forced myself to focus on what was in front of us.

I recognized the six lesser shadows as skogealv women. They dressed alike in flowing white gowns with long sleeves like my own, their expanse of straight blonde hair arranged on the trains of their skirts to keep from dragging on the ground itself.

But the central form remained in shadow. Only for a moment, as if she wanted me to know well that she could choose to remain there forever, and there was nothing I could do about it.

Then she chose to step into a patch of greenish sunlight filtered through the elm leaves above.

I didn't need to see her to know her, though. The cold sensation had already given her identity away.

"Princess Lianna," I said, putting my wand away. "Why do you stand in our way?"

She didn't answer me. She didn't even look my way. No, her eyes were unwavering in their regard of Thorbjorn.

"Lord of Villmark, you stray from our camp. Is there anything I might do to assist you?" she asked him, her hands clutching each other as if she desperately hoped the answer would be yes.

"We were only intending to walk a little in the woods," Thorbjorn told her. "That is not a matter in which either of us requires any assistance."

She laughed that bell-like laugh, as if his remark had been light-hearted flirting that delighted her. Which, I was pretty sure, was not how Thorbjorn had intended her to take it.

"Are these women here with you the intended brides?" he asked, sweeping his gaze at the six women in white who all stood silently next to the trunks of tall elms.

"They are. They are also my friends," Lianna said. Then she turned to point to each of them one at a time. "Bruna and Hella are sisters. Hanne, Sibylle and Myrta are cousins. And young Astri is a cousin of mine as well as a friend."

The women each nodded at the sound of their names, but none of them said a word or stepped closer to the sunny patch where Lianna stood with Thorbjorn.

My attention lingered longest on the one called Astri. She didn't look particularly younger than any of the others. I thought I could sense a coldness to her that was an echo of Lianna's. But I couldn't quite focus on it in my current state.

"In addition to solving your little murder, we're trying to find some missing men," I said to Lianna. "I don't suppose you'd know anything about that?"

She ignored me. But she did take a few steps closer to Thorbjorn, putting one hand on his arm as she leaned in to speak in a low, confidential tone.

"My father has put all of his trust in you. I only offer my help because I would very much like to see you succeed in your quest. Not that I don't think you can accomplish anything you wish without *my* aid. Still, I am at your disposal," she said. Her face was tipped up towards him, her emerald eyes fixed intently on first his eyes and then his mouth.

And my hands were curling into fists. I realized this and forced them to uncoil.

It's not like Thorbjorn was even responding to her at all. In fact, he took a step back from her before speaking.

"Perhaps you can illuminate something for me," he said conversationally.

"Anything," she said, trying again to close the distance between them once more.

But he took another step back again before asking, "We've heard that the six skogealv brides refused to cross the glade to take their place at the sides of the haugealv grooms," he said. "I'm just curious why they did that."

"I wish I could tell you," Lianna said with a frustrated, pouting sort of look on her face. "But they keep their own confidences. As I told you, I'm not one of their number. As a princess, I cannot be matched with just anyone."

"She knows you're not a prince, right?" I said to Thorbjorn. Because if she was going to keep talking to him as if I wasn't there... well, two could play that game.

Thorbjorn smirked but didn't answer me.

But my humor had already melted away. We were missing three of the shadows. The three cousins, Hanne, Sibylle and Myrta, were gone. I had lost track of them in my brain fog, somehow. But when had they slipped away? And to where?

"You know, I have friends among the haugealvs. Good friends. Friends who would be willing to help me, if I wanted to find a way to sneak you into their camp to see your brother," I heard Lianna say as I ducked around a few of the tree trunks, searching for where the women might have gone. But if they had slipped away, they had not only done it too quietly for me to notice, they had done it startlingly quickly.

That stand of evergreens behind me aside, everywhere else I could see quite a ways through the trees. If they had run away, they had done it at a sprint.

But even then, in those long white gowns, they would be so easy to spot among the greens and browns of the forest.

Not to mention, how could they even run in those outfits? My dress was slightly more practical, having no train, and my hair being barely shoulder-length was way more practical. And yet I doubted I could run through this forest fast enough to seem like I just disappeared.

"The brides are disappearing," I said to Thorbjorn, even as I noticed that two more were now gone. The sisters, Bruna and Hella. Only young Astri remained standing silently beside a tree, ignoring me but watching Lianna as she once more slid up closer to Thorbjorn.

"I can get you to your brother," Lianna was saying to him, even as he scowled down at her.

"I mean no offense, princess, but I do not wish to be in your debt," he said.

"I would ask nothing in return," she said.

"Even so," he said, shaking his head. "I will see my brother soon enough. And then my other questions will be answered. I hope these answers do not prove inconvenient to you, princess."

"How could they?" she said airily. "I only wish to see justice done. My father is determined to see our two alv tribes united, and I only wish for him to succeed. Well," she quickly amended with a blush, "I should very much like to see him succeed because of your help. He would owe you much for that. More than just the life of your brother."

It wasn't hard to work out what she wanted, but while I was

rolling my eyes over her lack of subtlety, the sixth bride faded into the woods without a sound or so much as a flash of white gown.

Was the ground swallowing them up?

Or were they just that good at woodcraft?

Maybe it was an alv thing. I knew the scouts were still around us. I could feel them watching, all the time. But I had yet to actually see one.

But this time, when Thorbjorn answered Lianna, he had my full attention. Because the undercurrent of humor that had carried through all of his dodges of her quips was gone now. No, her last remark had caused him real offense, and he was making no attempt at hiding it from her.

"There is no 'just' when it comes to the life of one of my brothers," he almost growled at her. "Now, princess, if you will excuse us, my volva and I were about to take a walk. And these woods are Villmark land. Your father may be king, but we need no king's permission to walk through our own woods."

"Indeed," Lianna said. I could hear her reaching for a bright, unbothered tone. But she wasn't quite achieving it.

"You have six brides who refuse to wed their intended grooms," Thorbjorn went on, still with that dangerous edge to his voice. "I can't help but notice that we Villmarkers are missing exactly six men."

"Six is three and three," Lianna said. "It could only be more auspicious if you were missing nine."

"Our men disappeared three on one night and three on the next," Thorbjorn said. "Does that strike you as… auspicious?"

"Surely there is someone among you who can answer that question better than I," she said, not quite looking at me.

But I had had enough of being even semi-ignored.

"Catch up when you're done here," I said to Thorbjorn, and picked a direction I was pretty sure was due south. I knew the evergreens were behind me, and the camp in the glade was on the far side of the evergreens, anyway. I gathered up my sleeves and started off through the woods.

Mjolner gave Thorbjorn an admonishing meow, and then followed after me.

"If you know the way, you should probably take the lead," I said to the cat. He meowed back at me, but not in a way that conveyed any meaning to me.

I wished Loke was there. He always knew what Mjolner was saying.

Although, being in a part of the world with a distinct paucity of doorways, he wasn't likely to randomly turn up.

I poked around in the woods with Mjolner for about a quarter of an hour before I heard the crashing sounds of a large body choosing speed over stealth to catch up to me. I turned to see Thorbjorn swatting at low-hanging branches in a rare show of irritability.

For a half a second, I thought he might be annoyed with me.

But from the way he rolled his eyes the minute he saw me, I knew it was the princess he had had enough of.

"She's not going to give up easily, I don't think," I said. I tried to sound like I was teasing him, but I couldn't quite pull it off.

It kind of hurt, watching someone else work that hard to win him over.

"She has no prospects," Thorbjorn said. "Her father's own rules mean no one in this world is worthy of being her husband."

"She wouldn't be the first woman who had to break her daddy's heart and live her own life," I grumbled.

"I only meant, the last time I met her, I had empathy for her position," he said. "I find I have less for her now."

"Really?" I asked. I mean, I knew why *I* didn't like her. But I knew I was biased.

"Really," he said. He chewed at his lip for a moment, and I just waited quietly until he worked out what he was thinking, what he wanted to say. "I know what you drew was only what we heard had happened. That she had found Tolkki already dead, just like you drew it."

"I want to say that I drew her standing over her victim, but I'm just not sure that's what happened," I said. "I didn't get that image. And there was no blood on her hands or on her gown or anything."

"Still, she's tied up in all of this somehow," he said. "Isn't she?" He looked at me, his eyes almost pleading with me to agree.

"I don't know," I had to admit. "She maybe knows more about the six missing men than she's telling us. She might even know more about your brother than she's saying. I mean, if you still think he was tricked into making this hostage agreement."

"I don't think he was tricked," Thorbjorn said. "I don't understand his reason, and I definitely think he got in over his head, but I don't think he was tricked."

"Okay, but I wouldn't put it past her to try," I said. "Unless you think she finds you more princely than your brothers?"

He actually blushed at that, deeply enough that he put up a hand to rub at the back of his neck and half turn away from me.

"Sorry. That was..." But I didn't know what that was. Too close to my truth?

I certainly found him more princely than his brothers.

But he just cleared his throat before turning back to me. "If she's involved in murder or even just in kidnapping, Ingrid, we absolutely have to have proof before we accuse her. And it has to be rock solid. Without that, anything we suspect, we have to keep very quiet and to ourselves."

"Royal protocol?" I guessed. "I mean, you did point out that they are in our lands."

"Still, it would be dangerous to forget that Alarik is not just a king. He's also a skogealv. To accuse his daughter..."

"No, I get it," I said with a sigh. "Like I said, I really think it's just the kidnapping she's not coming clean on. And if we can get those men back safe and sound, I don't see any reason to go to war over it."

"Don't joke," Thorbjorn said. "War is just what we're trying to avoid. It's just what my brother offered up his own life to avoid."

"I understand," I said. "I won't speak any suspicions in the camp. We can just gather all the information we can, then go over our potential suspects back at my cabin."

"That's a good plan," Thorbjorn said. "Where do we go from here?"

I looked at the forest all around us. I had wandered enough to feel pretty confident that if there was anything out there to be found, I would need a lot more people out looking for it.

"I think we should go back to the skogealv camp," I said. "They have Tolkki's body somewhere. I want to see it."

"Then we shall speak to the king," Thorbjorn said.

I slid my arm through his, and we walked back to the glade.

I just hoped that the princess had somewhere else to be. But I kind of doubted she did.

CHAPTER THIRTEEN

WE EMERGED from the forest to find the six skogealv grooms standing at the edge of the camp as if waiting for us to return. We were far west of the point where we had gone into the forest at the clump of evergreen trees, but we were still on the southern side of the camp.

Somewhere in the distance to the south and east of us was the path to Villmark. But at the moment, it felt very far away.

"Did you find what you sought?" Ilmar asked us as he and the other five shifted from slouching against tree trunks to standing tall and at the ready.

"Not as much as could be hoped," Thorbjorn said, but gestured for me to show the six men my sketchbook.

"We are looking for a knife like this one," I said, turning between the best of the drawings.

"Your brother had knives that were curved like that," Ilmar said, giving Thorbjorn an anxious look.

"They were curved, but they were not this knife," Thorbjorn said. Then he took my sketchbook from me to point at the runic-looking writing on the blade, the writing I couldn't quite read. "These are not Villmarker runes. Are they alvish?"

Ilmar and two of the others leaned in close to look, although they seemed reluctant to actually touch the pages. One of them, I thought perhaps it was Kallu, said, "It could be. It's not very well written. Like a child copying letters that they don't understand."

I felt my cheeks flush, although if I had indeed drawn alvish writing while in my magical fugue state, his description of it was actually pretty apt.

"There isn't enough that's clear to get a meaning out of it," Ilmar agreed. "But it certainly looks like it's meant to be alvish."

"Does anyone here carry such a knife?" Thorbjorn asked.

"We all have knives," Ilmar said, looking to the other five skogealv men. They all had knives at the back of their belts, but each had a straight blade. "I cannot think of anyone I've seen with a curved blade. Perhaps in the haugealv camp."

"Not that we're throwing accusations around," Kallu rushed to add, and Ilmar nodded his enthusiastic support of that statement.

"We want to help you in your investigation in any way we can, but we don't want to accuse... well, anyone who still may end up being family to any of us," Ilmar said.

"You still hope to marry?" I said. It sounded so insanely optimistic.

"That would depend on what actually happened to Tolkki," he said. "If he was killed by a haugealv plot, that would change things."

"It would almost be better if we found that the human had done it," one of the others grumbled. Then he flushed at Thorbjorn's hard glare. "My apologies. I spoke without thinking."

"We would like to see the body now, if we may," I said as I tucked my sketchbook away.

"Of course," Ilmar said with a little bow. "Tolkki has been laid out in his tent at the edge of the camp. He had no close family, but the king himself is sitting with him."

"We don't wish to disturb a private moment," Thorbjorn said.

"No, he will want you to do what you can before... well," Ilmar broke off with a quick glance towards the sun beating down hotly on the entire camp.

"Time does indeed grow short," Thorbjorn said.

Ilmar nodded, and the six men lead us to the far western edge of the camp. One tent, smaller than the others, was pitched a distance away.

I had smelled dead bodies before. They were never pleasant. And I really wasn't looking forward to the air inside that tent.

But the alvs are not without magic of their own. And these were skogealvs, lovers of earth and sky. So when two of the skogealv men pulled back the flaps of the tent, the scent that rushed out to meet me was the clean, dry smell of wildflowers.

And the sight inside that tent was of flowers everywhere. Great baskets of them were piled up all around the central bower, and the body itself was ringed in mounds of flowers so fresh they had yet to start wilting, even in all that heat.

Our skogealv guides declined to follow us into the tent, choosing instead to remain outside as an honor guard. So the only person in the tent besides the two of us and the dead body of Tolkki was the skogealv king Alarik.

He was standing on the far side of the bower with his head bowed, a bouquet of grass and flowers in his hands. But his hands were gripping it too tightly, crushing the stems and scattering petals all around his feet.

"We hope we're not disturbing you, King Alarik," Thorbjorn said as we stepped further into the tent.

"No, I was expecting you," he said. Then he dropped the rest of his bouquet to the ground and brushed the remains from the palms of his hands. "I understand you know what the murder weapon was."

I blinked, a bit startled to find he would know that. Had his daughter been and gone already? Because none of the grooms had come in with us, and no one else knew.

"I have a sketch, if you'd like to see it," I offered.

"No. I already know it's not a blade I would recognize," he said with a dismissive wave of his hand.

"Then you also know it was not my brother's blade," Thorbjorn said.

"Perhaps," the king said grudgingly.

"Or perhaps someone chose it to implicate Thoralv in something he didn't do," I suggested.

The king didn't look at me, and I thought for a moment that he, like his daughter, was going to carry on pretending like I wasn't even there.

But then he said, mostly to Thorbjorn, "I find it hard to fathom that someone would wish for us to blame your brother in the death of Tolkki. No one was expecting your brother to even be here."

"Perhaps it's just a coincidence then, and not proof against him," I said.

But he was back to ignoring me.

"May we take a closer look at the body?" Thorbjorn asked, gesturing to the form on the bower. The body was under a single sheer sheet of white silk, the features of his face just visible through the opaque fabric. But other than that sheet, it appeared to have been stripped naked.

"Of course," the king said, gesturing for Thorbjorn to move closer. "He was stabbed in the back. I will help you turn him over so you may see his wounds."

That was about the last job I would've expected the king to volunteer for, especially as six of his men were standing just outside the tent, ready to do his bidding without question. But he set to work at once, helping Thorbjorn move some of the flowers off of the tabletop until there was room enough to turn the body over.

I just stepped back out of the way and took out my sketchbook. Drawing while standing at an easel was one thing, but drawing as I held a book in the crook of my arm was definitely not my favorite. But I didn't want to risk drawing the king's ire by asking for a chair.

The two of them turned the body onto its front. Then the king caught up the end of the silk sheet and draped it over the body's buttocks, as if anxious to give him at least that much dignity in death.

Thorbjorn leaned in close to examine the back of the body, then stepped back to let me take his place.

I hated this part. I never got used to being in the same room as a dead body, let alone leaning in as close as possible to one. But I had to see. I had to draw.

Tolkki had been stabbed three times. The body had since been washed, but the wounds remained, never to heal.

"These wounds are all low on his back," Thorbjorn said to the king as I rapidly sketched the arrangement. In the close, floral-scented air of the tent, my headache was a constant throb. But even if I felt clear-headed, there was no way I could get into a proper fugue state with the king there with me. He was too much of a negative presence for that.

But I drew what Thorbjorn pointed out, as best as I could. It was a record. But it was not the magic I had hoped for.

"That is correct," the king said. But he was looking at Thorbjorn like he expected him to go on. Like he knew what Thorbjorn was going to say next.

Thorbjorn took a breath before pressing on. "The angle suggests they also came from below," he said.

"Tolkki was tall, even for a skogealv," the king said. "He was my champion. My finest warrior. He might not be so broad in the shoulders as your kind, but when he lived, he would've stood taller than you."

"I remember," Thorbjorn said softly.

"He must've been taken by surprise, then," I said, pausing in my drawing. "For a warrior to be stabbed from behind, it would have to be by surprise. Wouldn't it?"

"My brother did not do this," Thorbjorn said to the king. "Even if he were for some reason on his knees, he still wouldn't have stabbed Tolkki from behind."

"No, I never thought he did," the king said mildly. "But he gave his word. If the killer isn't identified by sundown tomorrow, he will pay the blood debt owed to the entire skogealv tribe." Then he gave Thorbjorn an inscrutable look before adding, "It seems to me a fair trade."

Thorbjorn scowled, and I sensed he was biting down on his own tongue to keep from answering.

But had Alarik meant to bait him? Was he trying to cause offense?

Or was he, in some backwards way that only made sense in his head, offering a compliment?

Not that it mattered. It wasn't a compliment Thorbjorn was prepared to receive.

"It's not a fair trade. At all," I said.

Thorbjorn shot me a look begging me to stop talking, but now it was my turn to ignore somebody. I kept my eyes on the king.

Who, maddeningly, looked like my words *amused* him.

"There is a great danger coming for Villmark. I've felt it for months. We will need every able-bodied Villmarker to stand shoulder to shoulder when that day comes. And you think taking one of our best away when he's needed most is a fair trade? To pay a blood debt he did nothing to accrue?"

The king just smirked at me, making a show of patiently waiting for me to be done.

But I wasn't done yet. "Do you think if you put him to death as you keep promising to do, that I'll just stand by for it?"

"Ingrid," Thorbjorn said warningly, but I stepped away from the hand that tried to grasp my arm.

"And it would all be so pointless!" I snapped at the king. "It wouldn't bring your warrior back to you. It would just deprive us of one of ours. And this danger that is coming, you know *exactly* what I'm talking about, don't you? Isn't it why you're all here, so far from the places you call home?"

"Ingrid, we should go," Thorbjorn said. He had turned to face me, turned so that his back was to the king. Which was probably against all kinds of protocol. But he clearly felt it was necessary.

So he could hit me with the full force of those pleading eyes of his.

It was really hard to tune him out. But my headache and my anger were both pounding too hard to let him sway me.

But then I heard the strangest sound. It took a moment to work out that it was the sound of the king chuckling.

"I've heard about you, Ingrid Torfudottir," he said, still laughing in that weird hyena-like, airless kind of way. "You come here from so very far away. And you have so much left to learn."

"Luckily, I have teachers," I said to him. "But I have nothing at all to learn from you."

Then I turned and stormed out of the tent. The six men outside were standing away from the door with the guilty air of people who didn't want to be caught eavesdropping.

I was well into the center of the open space between the two camps when Thorbjorn finally caught up with me. This time, I let him catch hold of my arm and pull me back.

Mostly because I didn't really know where I thought I was going next.

But there was still the awkwardness of not letting him do the talking like I'd promised.

"I'm not going to say I'm sorry for that," I said, gesturing at the skogealv camp, the king and all of it.

"I'm not asking you to," he said, stepping a little closer to me. Not that there was anyone close enough to overhear us in the middle of the grassy field. But he still lowered his voice before saying, "I was going to say thank you. For that."

"Oh," I said, and felt my cheeks heating up all over again. "Well. You're welcome."

I mean, I hoped I hadn't just put our village into open conflict with one and maybe two powerful and necessary allies.

But if I had, the warm glow in Thorbjorn's eyes as he beamed down at me would almost make it worth it.

CHAPTER FOURTEEN

THE TWO OF us were still standing together in the middle of the glade, just sort of smiling at each other, when I felt the prickles on the back of my neck that meant we were being watched.

Again.

Both kinds of alvs seemed to really enjoy spying from a distance.

But this was more intense than before, and I knew even before my eyes found her half-hidden by the side of one of the blue silk tents that it was Lianna who was watching us now.

Those prickles had been like shards of dry ice, painfully cold against the back of my neck.

"Come on," I said, taking Thorbjorn's hand.

"Where are we going?" he asked, looking down at my hand tugging his with amusement. As if I could ever pull him anywhere he wasn't perfectly willing to go.

"Anywhere she won't follow," I said. "I guess the haugealv camp to start."

"It looks like we're expected," Thorbjorn said. And, indeed, six young warriors were standing just inside the border of their camp. The six intended grooms, although this was the first time I'd seen them not intermixed with the six brides.

"Can we help you?" I asked them, trying not to sound as annoyed as I felt. But all of this being watched and being *expected* was starting to grate on me.

That, and it was just really stinking hot.

And the headache.

Always the headache.

"We were about to ask you the same question," one of them said. "We know you are investigating what happened here last night, but so far you've only been chumming around with the skogealvs. You haven't said a word to any of us save to our council."

"That wasn't deliberate," Thorbjorn said. "We started with the murder scene and then with the body. Those were both on the skogealv side of the camp. But if the six of you have a moment, we'd love to speak with you."

"Maybe in one of these tents?" I suggested. My gown was sticking to the sweat that was running down my back. It would almost be worth getting in eyeshot of Lianna again, just for another blast of that cold.

Almost.

"Certainly," the haugealv said, looking around. One of the others pointed to one of the larger tents, and the first nodded. Then they were all leading us into the shaded interior of one of the taller domes.

The tents were made of a heavier material than the skogealv silks, and the colors were darker as well. This made the interior quite dark, but also cool. Although part of this might have been because the tent wasn't just resting on the surface of the ground. They had dug down into the earth and set the tent atop it, making something that had looked too cramped in height for Thorbjorn to be comfortable inside of actually quite roomy.

And, while the air was still humid, it was more like the cool dampness of a cave. There were days where I would find that unpleasant.

But this was not that sort of day.

"I've sent a lad to find the intended brides for you," the haugealv, who seemed like their leader, told us as he gestured for us to sit on one of the long wooden benches that flanked the cold remains of a fire. "I'm sure you'll want to speak with them as well."

"Can we get names first?" Thorbjorn asked as I took out my notebook. As much as the haugealvs had more variety in their looks than the skogealvs, I was doomed to have trouble telling them apart as well, I could tell already. Everything inside that tent was just too much in shadow.

"I am Jokum," the leader said, then pointed at the others who had joined him all in a line along the bench opposite the one Thorbjorn and I were sharing. "This is my brother Gael and my brother Sejr. Niilo, Yanik and Dres are also brothers."

"Well, half-brothers," the one called Niilo said with a grin. "Same father, three different mothers."

"And you were all volunteering to marry women from the skogealv camp?" I asked. I was still having trouble with the idea of having twelve weddings happen all at once and none of them being even a little coerced.

But they all looked at each other and shrugged. "For our two tribes to live in peace, it was necessary to make the gesture," Jokum said. "For my part, I didn't find the prospect of marrying Hella any sort of hardship."

The others chuckled and muttered a few other of the skogealv women's names.

"Wait," I said, pencil at the ready. "Can you tell me the names of your intendeds? It might be important."

"I don't see any reason to refuse," Jokum said to the others.

"I was meant to wed Bruna," Gael said.

"Sibylle," Sejr said.

"Hanne," said Niilo.

"Myrta," said Yanik.

And at the end of the line, the one called Dres said, "Astri is my intended."

"But they didn't come forth when summoned, did they?" Thorbjorn said as I wrote all this down as well as I could in the dim light. "Any idea why?"

"It was all a bit rushed," Niilo said with a shrug. "They were called, but it wasn't like they were refusing to come out. It was more like they weren't ready yet or something."

"It was their wedding day," Dres said. "It's not unusual for that to involve... extra grooming."

"So it was only a few moments between their absence being noted and the body being found?" I asked. My pencil was making soft scratching noises across the page, but I wasn't taking notes so much as sketching without looking.

I mean, I would've been hard pressed to sketch while looking in such a dark interior. It was just that with a pencil in my hand and paper as well, drawing was something that was bound to happen. I could only hope I'd come up with something interesting when I was back out in the light once more.

"That's how I remember it," Jokum said, and the others nodded at his questioning look to them. "They were still being looked for when we heard the princess scream. Then everything after that was just chaos."

"And then your brothers turned up, and there was more chaos," Niilo said.

"I heard they stopped the fighting," Thorbjorn said.

"Eventually," Jokum said. "It took a bit for the king to stop raging and actually listen to what your brother was saying."

"And once he listened, he insisted that your brother swear that Tolkki's death would be paid for," Niilo said. "Which he did, but by that point it was pretty clear no weddings were going to be happening. Not yet, anyway."

"We know our brides are still over there," Jokum said. "They won't cross the open field to talk to us, but we've seen them moving through the camp."

"And in the woods," Dres put in. "They spend a lot of time in the woods."

"Well," Jokum said with a dry chuckle. "They *are* skogealvs."

"Do you know anything about our missing men?" I asked. At their blank looks, I added, "Six Villmarker men have gone missing. That was what Thorulv and Thoralv were doing here in the first place. They didn't come to break up a fight. Or to kill a man, whatever some might think. They were looking for our missing men."

"I know nothing of that," Jokum said, but he looked pensive as he rubbed at the back of his neck. "Six, you say?"

"Six," I said. "They were young men. Five were unmarried, but one has a wife in Villmark."

"Wait, what are you saying?" Niilo asked, looking as much at his brothers and the other haugealvs as at me and Thorbjorn.

"Well, it *would* make sense," Dres said. "They chose other grooms for themselves. That's why they didn't come when summoned."

"I still say not enough time passed to be sure they weren't *intending* to come," Jokum said.

"Have you seen anything in the woods?" Thorbjorn asked.

"Well, no, but they keep to the woods on their side of the glade," Niilo said. "We wouldn't be welcomed there. And the scouts on both sides are keeping a close eye on all of us. No one leaves the confines of either camp."

"You know that for sure?" I asked.

"Every scout on their side has a corresponding scout on our side," Jokum said. "It would be very difficult to avoid being seen by two sets of eyes. We all take a watch, and we never get matched with the same skogealv scout twice. It would be very difficult for anyone to collude in those circumstances."

"Very difficult," Niilo stressed.

"And yet Tolkki was killed, very close to camp," I said. "And no one saw it happen."

"You're right," Dres said. "We can't be sure of anything. Not really."

"We are looking for a weapon," Thorbjorn said, nudging me with his elbow. I turned back to the appropriate pages in my sketchbook. I could barely see the details myself, but the haugealvs studied them intently without even needing to squint.

"It looks like one of your brother's knives," Jokum said, but then added before Thorbjorn could object, "but it isn't. He had both knives on him when he turned himself in to us. There wasn't a drop of blood on either blade, nor anywhere on his person."

"The ground where the body had been found was soaked," Niilo said. "And the wounds were deep. No one could stab a man like that and not get drenched in his blood. Or, at least, I don't see how it could be done."

"Lianna found the body," I said.

"Princess Lianna," Thorbjorn corrected me.

"Princess Lianna," I said, not quite rolling my eyes at the title. "She found the body. How bloody was she?"

"She was wearing white," Jokum said, but looked to the others for confirmation.

"It was a pale green and white gown," Niilo said with a frown of concentration. "The hem in front was soaked from where she had bent over him. But the rest of her was quite clean."

"And she was wearing long sleeves?" I asked, indicating my own sweeping sleeves, no longer as white as they had been that morning.

"Longer than those," Jokum said. "But not a drop of blood on them that I saw."

"Are you accusing—?" Niilo started to say, but Thorbjorn cut him off abruptly.

"No! We are certainly not accusing the princess of anything," he said. "We are just gathering facts. About, I guess, time of death?"

He gave me a questioning look, but I just shrugged. I didn't need him to explain to me the need for convincing proof before we pointed fingers. But I had to admit I was trying to accuse Lianna.

Not just because I didn't like her personally. And not even because of the intense cold she radiated every time I was near her. That warmth-sucking, life-draining chill felt like a kind of evil to me.

But I had to admit, she felt like a far stronger suspect than anyone else did.

So far, the only other person with any connection to Tolkki at all was the king. And as much as I didn't really like him either, I didn't think he'd done this.

Just to start, I didn't think he'd feel the need to hide anything he ever chose to do.

But his daughter might.

Although with their engagement being the very slightest of hypotheticals, I wasn't sure what her motivation was either.

I sighed, turning over the pages of my sketchbook. But all I had added since going into the haugealv tent was pictures of barrow-wights like from the old folk tales. Which I really hoped none of the men sitting before me had seen. I didn't know how they felt about barrow-wights, but it was just possible that conflating haugealvs with barrow-wights might be offensive to them.

I turned to a blank page, but only twirled my pencil through my fingers idly.

"Do we have any other questions for these men?" Thorbjorn asked me.

"Not at the moment," I said with a sigh.

"We'll let you talk with the brides then," Jokum said as he got to his feet.

"And they've brought food with them," Niilo announced as he headed out the tent door.

My stomach heard his words and answered with a loud rumble. It had been too many hours since that toast, and the thought of the eggs I had decided not to make was really haunting me now.

But Thorbjorn seemed unmoved by the thought or even the growing smell of food. He just looked at me with sadness clear in his eyes. "Half a day gone," he said softly to me. "Half a day gone and we still know so little."

"We're gathering facts," I told him. "It's not unusual for me to put facts together into theories when I'm meditating or even sleeping. We still have time."

He nodded and tried to smile as if heartened by my words.

But I didn't think he really was.

CHAPTER FIFTEEN

THE SIX HAUGEALV women we had seen around the fire that morning came into the tent and arranged themselves in a row on the bench opposite of Thorbjorn and me.

But a seventh young woman also came into the tent. She was far younger than the others, just barely past adolescence, with round cheeks that made her look younger still.

I was no judge of alv ages, but the sight of her, with so many soft signs of childhood only recently passed clear in her features, made me realize for the first time I had seen no children at all in the camp.

"Are there more haugealvs and skogealvs than are in this glade?" I asked Thorbjorn.

"Of course," he said. "The old and the young, Valeria aside, don't travel outside of their homes far west and north of here."

"Well, but that's why—" one of the women across from us started to say, before the other five quickly shushed her. She fell silent at once, but her cheeks blazed scarlet.

"Would you care for some food, volva and Valkisson?" the young woman asked. She was holding a massive wooden platter that was loaded with crusty rolls of bread, wedges of cheese, and sliced apples. I reached out for it, then remembered Thorbjorn's warning just in time. I let my hands drop back onto my lap with almost audible regret.

"We thank you, but—" Thorbjorn started to say.

But the young woman interrupted him before he could finish. "This food, our hospitality, imparts no obligation on your part. In fact, I — I mean, *we*—already owe you and yours a tremendous debt. Accepting this food would only be a gesture of goodwill between our peoples. It does not even begin to repay what we owe."

She spoke all in a rush, her cheeks flushing redder and redder with each word. The other six women were frowning at her, but with a certain fond indulgence in their demeanor rather than true censure.

I chewed at my lip but waited for Thorbjorn to answer her.

"Very well, young haugealv. We accept your gesture of goodwill, hopefully with as much grace as it was extended," he said at last.

I murmured thanks of my own even as I reached towards that platter. The apples looked a little too green for my tastes, but I helped myself to bread and cheese.

Then she offered me a tall wooden mug filled with cold, clear water. I drank it down in very impolite gulps, then held it back out for her to refill it from a leather skin she wore hanging from her belt. I took a more delicate sip from this one, then smiled my deepest thanks at her.

Not that the young alv woman noticed. No, her eyes never strayed from Thorbjorn. But this wasn't in a creepy way like when Lianna did it. It was more like she was trying really hard not to go all fangirl on him.

Perhaps she remembered him from when he had visited the haugealvs before? If it had been as many years ago as Thorbjorn had said, I guessed she would've been a tween at the time.

Unless alvs aged more slowly than humans, even as children. Maybe she had looked just the same, but was marveling at how much older he was.

I made a mental note to ask Thorbjorn so many questions later, and turned my attention to the women sitting across from us, patiently waiting as we helped ourselves to the food.

"Thank you, Alfhild. You may go," one of the women said when Thorbjorn and I had both taken enough. Alfhild managed a little curtsey despite the weight of her still laden platter, then swept back out of the tent.

"You've seen the men in the other camp? The grooms, I mean," said the woman whose cheeks were still tinged red from whatever she had earlier been about to say.

"We have," Thorbjorn said with a quick glance at me. I gave him the smallest of nods, and he turned back to her to add, "If it cheers you to hear it, they are still willing to marry all of you, despite everything that's happened."

"Thank you, that is heartening to hear," the one who had thanked Alfhild said. Then she shifted on the bench, half-turning towards the others. "My name is Adla. The others here with me are Kikki, Zenia, Berta, Maija and Heidi."

"No sisters among you?" Thorbjorn asked between bites of cheese and bread.

"No, none of us are sisters. Although we're all cousins of one sort or another," Adla said. Kikki of the scarlet cheeks nodded her agreement with this.

"We understand you picked which of the skogealv grooms you each wanted for yourselves," Thorbjorn said. "Can we ask their names?"

"I chose Ilmar," Adla said. "Kikki chose Edel, Maija Olai, Zenia Uki, Heidi Caro, and Berta chose Kallu."

I set my food aside long enough to scrawl all those names down. Then I took another drink of water, so grateful that my headache was finally easing.

Although the cool interior of the tent helped too.

"You're not worried what life will be like living among the skogealvs?" I asked. "They seem..." I fought to find a word besides *cold*, but came up empty. "Different," I finished, lamely.

"I wouldn't fancy the idea of wearing those gowns they favor all day, every day," Adla said with a wrinkle of her nose. "But Ilmar already promised me he had no desire for me to mold myself into a skogealv woman."

"We are warriors, the same as are men," Kikki put in. "The skogealv women can certainly fight if they need to, but they only train as a formality."

"So with these watches as scouts paired up with skogealvs doing the same on the other side?" I asked leadingly.

"We all take turns on this side, men and women alike," Adla said. "They do not."

"But we won't be required to stay among the skogealvs if it doesn't suit us," Kikki said. "We will remain wed in name, and any children we produce will be welcome in either home, but we don't have to stay if we choose not to."

"I guess that makes it easier, marrying a stranger," I said. Although the idea was still giving me the shivers.

"The skogealvs, men and women both, can come across as cold and remote," Adla said with a musing look on her face, "but in the little time we've spent with them, they don't seem all bad."

"Well, except for—" Kikki started to say.

"Yes, except for him," Adla agreed.

"Who are we talking about?" Thorbjorn asked. "Not one of the grooms, I hope?"

"We probably shouldn't," Kikki said lowly to the others.

"It's a little late for that, now that you've brought him up," Zenia, who was sitting next to her, said. But she didn't sound angry. More like someone who enjoyed teasing her blush-prone friend.

"We don't need to worry about him now, surely," Adla said. "We did worry, before. He seemed very likely to be foisted off on one of us. But I guess none of us were quite good enough for him."

"Tolkki," I guessed.

"Tolkki," they agreed.

"He was more than cold. He was *cruel*," Maija said in the barest of whispers. As if she were still afraid he would overhear her.

"Cruel how?" Thorbjorn asked, leaning forward in sudden interest. "Was it just cutting words, or did he do something?"

"I suppose it was just the former," Adla said with a sigh.

"I don't know," Maija said. "It always felt like he was on the verge of… something. He would take your arm, but he'd squeeze just a little too hard. Or he'd look at you, and you knew in your bones you absolutely didn't want to see what was going on inside his mind."

"He made me feel… unclean, I guess," Zenia said.

"We stayed together in pairs," Kikki said. "Just to be sure none of us were alone with him."

"And we all watched out for Alfhild," Adla said. "His eyes were on her far too much. She was never considered for bridal duty. Too young. Well, she's an adult, but still. It was made very clear which of us were volunteering and which were not. And yet Tolkki watched Alfhild all the time, and with this hungry sort of look."

She shivered at the memory, and I found myself shaking away a chill of my own. Like the creeps were contagious in the same way a yawn was.

"Did anyone else worry about Alfhild?" Thorbjorn asked. "A brother or father or uncle, perhaps?"

I nodded at the path his question was taking towards finally finding a motive, but said nothing out loud.

"No, she has no close family. Although, like the rest of us, she's a sort of cousin," Adla said.

"I think she's closest to me," Kikki said, touching her fingertips as if counting. "Third cousin? I think. I'd need to be home with the old scrolls to be sure."

"That's why we were looking out for her, the six of us," Maija said. "She was alone here otherwise."

"You didn't tell anyone else?" Thorbjorn asked.

"We didn't want to make trouble," Kikki said. "I mean, once we knew none of us were going to have to refuse to marry him and risk making a scene. And Alfhild wasn't a volunteer. So it was just a matter of keeping her safe until this was all in the past and he was far away from her."

"You all carry weapons," Thorbjorn said with a glance towards me.

I pulled out my sketchbook and showed the pages to them. "Do you know this knife?"

"No," Adla said. But there were too many glances between the women for me to take that as a final answer.

"Does it suggest anything to you?" I asked. "I know the lettering is wrong. I don't speak your tongue, let alone write it. But if it prompts anything at all in your minds, it would be helpful for us to know."

"The curved blade," Adla said at last, tracing the shape with a fingertip before giving Thorbjorn a desperate sort of look.

"It is similar to the blades my brother Thoralv carries," he said with a resigned sigh.

"No," she said, then shook her head. "I mean, yes, obviously. But that wasn't what I was thinking."

"Someone else has a blade like this?" he asked, his eyes bright with the beginnings of hope.

"I don't know this knife specifically," Adla said with maddening slowness. But I resisted the urge to try to hurry her words.

"Some of the skogealv women carry knives like this," Maija said at last. As if her patience gave out quicker than mine.

"Really?" Thorbjorn said, taking the sketchbook to examine the drawing closely, as if seeing it for the first time.

"Not all of them," Kikki said. "But some do."

"I've never seen a skogealv woman with a blade," Thorbjorn said, not quite doubtfully, but definitely on the edge.

"No, it's true. Some carry them," Adla insisted. "They don't like to be seen with them. Not even by their own men. They take this weird pride in knowing how to fight but never, ever being prepared for one."

"Ridiculous skirts with trains," Kikki grumbled. "Ridiculous hair. Ridiculous sleeves!"

I didn't make a move, but her eyes were drawn to my own admittedly ridiculous sleeves, and her cheeks went deeply crimson all over again.

"They carry these inside their sleeves?" Thorbjorn asked. But even less doubtfully than before. It was like I could hear the whirring of gears in his mind as he imagined just how that could be done. "This would have to be smaller than I imagined."

"With nothing there but the knife itself, it's hard to convey scale," I said.

"I was not finding fault with your artwork, Ingrid," he said. "Only with my own assumptions. I knew for a fact it wasn't my brother's blade. And yet I kept picturing the size of his blades."

"It's probably only about this long," Adla said, holding her fingers about six inches apart. "But if they train the way they claim to, it would be a matter of knowing precisely where to strike."

"They could kill someone with only three hits," I guessed.

"Yes, in the right circumstances. I think that sounds correct," Adla said, and the others nodded in mute agreement.

"So you spent some time with the skogealv women?" I asked.

"Not a lot. But a little," Adla said.

"The first three nights, before the negotiations bogged down, there was a lot of mingling between the two camps," Kikki said. "I don't know how many volunteers they would've gotten for brides or grooms if we hadn't known each other at least a little from sharing meals and drinking together around the fire those first nights."

"Did you get any sense from the skogealv women that they were repulsed by Tolkki the way you all were?" I asked.

They looked at each other as if carefully considering their answer. But in the end, Adla shook her head, and the others quickly followed up with shakes of their own.

"No, he was more considered off limits, I would say," Adla said. "They didn't seem to be the focus of his attention ever."

"Not that they felt slighted or anything," Kikki added. "It was more just like they accepted it as the nature of things. They didn't even question it."

"Because he was meant to marry Princess Lianna?" I asked.

They shrugged. "I guess," Adla said.

"And did you get any sense of whether she herself wanted that?" I asked.

"The princess?" Adla asked, surprised. At my nod, she looked to the others before saying, "We never really spoke with her at all. No, when all of us young people were mixing together, she was always very firmly at her father's side. She had no interest in any of us at all, men or women."

"Or Tolkki, for that matter," Kikki said. "And he never looked at her in any kind of warm way, either. For two people meant to be married someday, they had an epic level of disregard for each other. It's actually kind of impressive."

"Was," Zenia corrected her. "It was kind of impressive. But he's dead now. And we're all still unwed because of it."

"And all that that implies," Kikki added darkly.

But I didn't see any point in pressing for the answers to my bigger questions. Like why they were here, and what they were negotiating with each other for. I already knew they wouldn't answer.

I looked to Thorbjorn, and he gave a little shake of his head, agreeing in the lack of point. They weren't going to tell us anything, except possibly by mistake. And as much as I wanted to know what was going on, this didn't feel like something I needed to get information about by any means possible.

But I also suspected that Thorbjorn had a pretty good idea of what was going on. Only we had to leave the camp before he would tell me anything.

"I think it's time to get back to my cabin," I said. "I'm a little worried where Mjolner popped off to. He was with me in the woods, but he's gone now."

"I would bet good money he's off with Loke somewhere," Thorbjorn said, but even as he did he slapped his hands to his knees and levered himself up from the bench. "But I agree. We've done all we can here."

"For now," I said, with a look at the six women. They were clearly anxious for us to leave so they could compare their own notes.

I only hoped if they had any real suspicions, they would give us a hint. Because so far, I knew nothing more than I had the minute I had even heard there had been a murder.

And time was running out.

CHAPTER SIXTEEN

THORBJORN and I were back at my cabin in the woods by midafternoon. I could see that his energy was flagging long before our walk back from the glade ended. I didn't know just how far away he had been when Mjolner had found him, but given that he had arrived at dawn, he must've gotten up and started hiking home in the middle of the night.

Not that it was easy to convince him that he needed a nap.

"We need to talk this through," he said, even as he fumbled in the simple act of sitting down in one of the chairs around my dining table.

"I need to think and draw some more first," I said. "I need more to go on before talking is going to be helpful. And as much as I appreciate it when you stand over me when I draw at crime scenes, I'm home now. I'm perfectly safe here. So just let me get into my civilian clothes, and then I want you to lie down on my bed for at least a few hours. Until dinner. Then we can eat and talk."

He took a long time thinking this over. Clearly, because he was so exhausted. But I let him come to his own conclusion.

He nodded, then went outside to give me a moment's privacy.

The cozy one-room cabin had a few drawbacks that hadn't been apparent all the days I had spent there alone. I mean, the only room with any privacy was the little bathroom built off the north side of the round hut. And there was not enough room in there to change my clothes unless I stood in the tub itself.

And it wasn't a large tub. More like a Japanese style soaking tub than anything. In the gown I was in, the whole process of changing would just be too awkward in that little space.

So I had to kick him out. And close the cabin shutters.

I hung my volva gown from one of the tall bedposts. It needed a little mending and a lot of cleaning before I put it away again, neither of which I'd have time for before I had to wear it again back in the glade.

The countdown clock of Thoralv's remaining time never ceased ticking in the back of my mind.

But it was like changing out of the long sleeves and full skirts into cutoff shorts and a tank top somehow cleared my mind. Or maybe it was just finally having total access to all the water I could ever want while enjoying the shade my own roof provided.

And after I pulled the hair up off the back of my neck into a high ponytail, I felt even better. I hadn't appreciated just how sweaty I'd gotten.

"Okay, time for you to rest," I announced as I opened the front door. I had my art bag with me, prepared to settle on one of the many log benches that dotted the open area around my cabin, muse over everything I'd seen that day, and let my pencil draw whatever it willed.

It took me a minute to find Thorbjorn, as he had gone around the curve of the cabin wall to the well out back. In the time I had taken to change my clothes and put up my hair, he had scrubbed himself clean in the cold well water. Both of his tunics were hanging clean but dripping from my clothesline, and his newly washed boots were sitting in the shade nearby to air dry.

Which, yeah, meant he was currently barefoot and shirtless. And his hair was dripping wet.

And I knew exactly what my pencil willed to draw in that moment. Which wasn't going to be helpful for the investigation.

But this was an image that was going to be hard to put out of my mind. I mean, I was pretty sure it had burned in there permanently.

"You're sure I can't be of any help?" he asked me as he ran his hands through his freshly combed hair.

I had to swallow a few times before I managed to get out the words, "Positive. You should go rest. I have a feeling once we start talking after dinner, it might be a late night."

"I would feel better if Mjolner were here," he said, but there was still no sign of my cat.

"He comes and goes... well, I was going to say as he wishes, but that's not quite right," I said.

"He comes and goes as he's needed," Thorbjorn said with a nod. "I can trust in that."

"Yes. But also, I'm not in any danger here. And I will be just outside. If anything does happen where I need you, you'll hear me," I said.

"Very well. But wake me in an hour," he said.

I nodded, carefully keeping my facial expression completely sincere.

But there was no way I was waking him up in anything less than two hours. Not with those dark smudges under his eyes.

Once he went into the cabin, shut the door, and was safely out of my sight, I sat down on the nearest bench. Or, more accurately, I collapsed onto it. My knees were a little weak.

I wanted to blame all the walking we had done that day.

But then I realized I was already drawing, and what I was drawing was specifically what I had known I was going to draw. Thorbjorn, as I had just seen him a moment before.

I don't like to praise my own skills, but it was a very vivid likeness. I could feel my cheeks heating all over again just looking at it.

I folded the page in half and tried to put the image out of my mind once more.

Which, after a moment's perusal of my earlier drawings, wasn't as difficult as I had feared.

Mostly because those other drawings were so maddeningly vague.

Curved knife aside, there were no details I could consider any kind of clue or lead.

So I turned to the next blank page in my sketchbook and just started drawing in a free association sort of way. The tents arranged around the glade. The king and his daughter. The brides and grooms of the skogealv camp. The brides and grooms of the haugealv camp.

The haugealvs struck me as the more likable of the two tribes. But once I had properly met and spoken with them, the skogealv grooms had been a little stiff but not entirely unfriendly.

It was only the skogealv brides I had never gotten to know. They had loomed over me, but they had yet to really speak with me.

I wished I had thought of that before we'd walked all the way home. But I had to give myself a bit of a break. It was only now that my mind was once more clear and pain-free that I could appreciate just how debilitating that brain fog had been all day in the glade.

But as remote as they were, I drew the skogealv brides as well as the others, hoping that telling details would emerge from my subconscious mind.

But I had no luck with that.

When the sun started to set, I only noticed because it was getting harder and harder to see the page before my eyes. Then I realized I was drawing the missing men. The second set of three I knew well enough to draw from memory, but the first three to go missing I hadn't thought I knew at all.

But I had sketches of them now, and my gut insisted I had captured their likenesses faithfully.

Not sure what to make of that, I put the book and pencils away and then went into the cabin to find something to put together for dinner. I had some left over roast chicken in the icebox. Which was literally an old-fashioned icebox, as my cabin had no electricity of any kind. I had to light a camping lantern to see by as I put a pot of water on the camp stove, then set about making a chicken pasta salad.

"Ingrid, it's very dark," Thorbjorn chided me, making me jump. He had been sleeping when I'd come into the cabin, but now he was in the little kitchen area with me. He must've gotten out of bed and walked across the cabin with a cat's grace. Although even Mjolner made more noise than that.

"Sorry, I got caught up," I said.

"Any clues?" he asked. I could tell he was trying not to sound too eager, but I still felt bad when I had to shake my head no.

"Everything I drew just confirms the conclusions I already had come to," I said as I stirred the cooked pasta and chopped chicken together with a few other ingredients I had scraped together from my nearly empty pantry. I had been so well-stocked nine... no, ten days ago. Now, as usual, I really needed to do some shopping.

"We can't accuse the princess without solid proof," he said.

"I know. You said," I sighed. I spooned pasta salad into two bowls, then handed one to Thorbjorn along with a fork. Then we sat together at my little table, the lantern hissing softly between us.

"Despite how secretive and evasive they're being, I think we can feel sure that whatever you sense coming for Villmark has already driven them from their customary homes," Thorbjorn said between bites. "Usually they stay far away from each other, and far away from Villmark. For them both to be so close together, and so close to us, something significant has changed in the wilds."

"I wish I knew what it was," I said. "Vague feelings of a coming dread make it really hard to know what to prepare for."

"I'm hoping once we've sorted this all out, and Thoralv is free, we can ask them again what has happened," he said. "It's possible they are moving away from something they understand as little as we do, but being closer to it, they feel it more intently."

"Or they feel it more intently because they are inherently more in touch with such things than we are?" I asked.

Thorbjorn made a conceding nod, but said nothing. I got up to bring the rest of the pasta salad over to the table to refill his already empty bowl.

"You may be right," he said. "But I'm also hopeful that they will share what they know after we've resolved things. It *is* possible they know something that could be helpful to us. That's why it's so important we handle this delicately. There is more on the line than just my brother's life."

"Okay, but for now, I'm just going to focus on that. It's a more immediate need, but also a more clear-cut one," I said.

"The two alv camps are trying to find a way to live in closer proximity to each other," Thorbjorn said. "I can think of no other thing which would require exchanging brides to resolve it. If either of them were even considering a plan that would involve one or both of them moving farther away, they wouldn't be exchanging daughters and sons to seal the deal."

"That makes sense," I said. "Of course, I don't really understand their culture."

"The differences between them and us are few and subtle," Thorbjorn said after some thought. "That only makes the differences harder to spot, and even of more consequence, I think."

"I agree we can't accuse Lianna of murder. I didn't see her stabbing him when I drew that picture, and even if I had, that wouldn't really be proof in the eyes of the king, I'm sure."

"He would be willing to hear you out, perhaps. But he wouldn't take any action without something he could see for himself," Thorbjorn said.

"I *do* think she knows where the Villmarker men are," I said. I pushed my empty bowl aside, then started turning the pages of my sketchbook, looking at the newest drawings. The sketches I had done of the Villmarker men all showed such anxious looks on their faces. But maybe that was me projecting my own mood on the drawings.

"We don't have any leads to follow for the murder itself. But maybe finding the men will lead us to the killer? I know it's a long shot. But can we ask about that without actually accusing her? I mean, if we can get the king at least curious enough to look into it himself, maybe they can be found."

"That would be tricky," Thorbjorn said. "Again, getting the king's assistance in a search of the woods will be easier if we can name the killer first."

"Maybe I'll dream something useful," I said, although I couldn't even feign confidence in those words. "But somehow I think my dreams are just going to be of that skogealv princess and her cold, cold eyes."

I shivered just at the memory of her glaring at me.

"A lot of that is just part of being a skogealv," Thorbjorn said. He gestured towards the sketchbook I had stopped paging through, and I nodded my consent for him to examine the drawings. He slid the book to his side of the table, then started at the beginning, with my drawings based on what Thorulv had tried to tell me that morning.

But he kept talking even as he leaned forward and tipped the book from time to time to better catch the light from the camping lantern. "The skogealvs all are cold and aloof compared to the haugealvs, let alone compared to humans. Being considered royalty from birth has isolated Lianna, even from the other skogealvs. She has no siblings, only distant cousins, and I think no true friends."

"I thought you said you didn't have any empathy for her?" I asked. I winced a little at how snotty my own words sounded in my ears, but Thorbjorn didn't look up from his careful inspection of my drawings.

"Less than before, but not quite zero," he said. Which was fair. I doubted Thorbjorn was capable of feeling zero empathy for anyone, human or otherwise.

I mean, I'd seen him treat trolls with kindness.

"I suppose I should be the bigger person and try to see things from her point of view," I said, but I was still kind of grumbling. "Or maybe that would be a mistake? Trying to empathize with her might make me less impartial to her. I mean, if she really is a suspect?"

Thorbjorn said nothing. He just looked up at me, one eyebrow raised high.

Yeah, I was reaching.

"Fine. I admit I don't like her," I said, crossing my arms and slouching in my chair in a way that I was pretty sure Loke would admire. But it was annoying even talking about her.

"To be fair, I don't think she likes you either," Thorbjorn said. I knew he was teasing, but I was still feeling cross.

"Of course she doesn't. She wants you all to herself, and as the volva you stand beside, I will always be there. She *hates* that."

I maybe took a little too much delight in that observation. But as I said the words, I knew just how true they were. That was what most of her icy stares had been about. There was no doubt about that.

But Thorbjorn looked up at me, his hands still holding the pages of my sketchbook. Perhaps it was the dim light from the lantern sitting on the table between us that made him hard to read, but the expression on his face in that moment was completely inscrutable to me. As was the tone in his voice when he said, "Is that what I am to you? The man who stands beside you as you fulfill your office?"

"Of course not—" I started to say.

Then I realized he was grinning at me. No, beaming at me. Like something had just made him the happiest man alive.

Which, given what I had just sort of accidentally implied, didn't exactly make any sense.

But then I saw the page he was holding down flat with his hands.

The page I had so carefully folded out of sight before.

"Oh. That," I said, even as something birdlike started fluttering around inside my chest. "I can explain that?"

But he just shut the book. Carefully, so as not to crumple my very detailed drawing of him.

"I really don't think you need to. Do you?" he asked.

Then he was reaching for me around the little table, and I was reaching for him, but it was our lips that met first.

And he was right. I really, really didn't need to explain what I'd been feeling when I had done that drawing.

Because he was feeling it too. And I was suddenly warm in a way that had nothing to do with the sticky July night.

And I knew that Lianna had no power to ever make me feel cold again. Because I knew where my warmth would always come from.

And I knew now it would always be there.

CHAPTER SEVENTEEN

My dreams that night were totally abstract, dominated by visions of the vend rune everywhere. Not like a sharp-edged capital P, that would be a little *too* abstract, but like a triangular flag slapping in the wind. Flags around my cabin, flags around my home in Villmark, flags around the mead hall down in Runde. So many flags.

Then I woke to see Thorbjorn sleeping beside me, and I realized my dream was right. I was feeling a lot of joy and connection at the moment.

Like, a lot.

But there was still a murder to solve and a brother to save. And we only had until sundown to do it.

As if he felt me watching him, Thorbjorn opened his eyes and gave me a sleepy smile. "Good morning," he said.

But I couldn't quite muster up that optimistic of a response. So instead, I said, "We need to get back to the glade."

"You dreamed something?" he asked, sitting up at once. He went from groggy to alert inside of the blink of an eye, and without so much as a sip of coffee.

"I had very lovely, but not particularly helpful, dreams," I admitted. "No, I was just thinking. All the things you say will be easier if we solve the murder first, I think we need to do some of them the hard way."

"What do you mean?" he asked with a frown.

"I don't see a way to solve this without talking to the most important witness. Your brother," I said.

"No," he said, shaking his head. "I mean, I agree. We need to do that. But there's no way either side is going to go for it. He swore an oath, and the wording of that oath precluded us talking to him. The king and the council not only won't budge, they, by their own rules, can't. I mean, it would be like asking them to hold their breaths until sunset. They just *can't*."

"So humans running into trouble with alv promises isn't really about the alvs trying to trick them into something?" I asked.

"Sometimes, I suppose it is. But mostly, the wording of the promises that bind alvs is older magic. Older than the alvs themselves. It can't be altered."

"Binding like legal contracts, only more so," I said. "Still, I don't see a way forward that doesn't start with asking for that."

"Okay," he said. "But what do we do after they say no?"

"Ask for the king's assistance in finding our men," I said. "He doesn't think the two things are related, right? So why wouldn't he agree to help? I mean, because of the promises made, our time is tied up. His people can spare a few hours to search the woods."

"We can certainly ask," Thorbjorn said, but he didn't sound like he thought it would be a fruitful endeavor.

But we really had nothing else to try.

After a hasty breakfast that ended with my tea and his coffee in travel mugs, we started the hour-plus hike from my cabin to the glade.

There was still no sight of Mjolner, but the moment I stepped outside and made a quick search of the sculpture-cluttered yard around my cabin, I had a flash of an image from my dreams the night before.

He had been walking with Loke. They were in trees, but I couldn't tell more than that, not even if they were near Villmark or were somewhere else entirely.

They had also been surrounded by brightly colored vend rune flags, but I was pretty sure that was a random, unrelated dream element.

I wasn't particularly happy about getting back into my volva gown. The more I wore it, the less it felt like something I should be wearing. My hope that it would make me feel more like a proper volva, and a person to be respected, was fading the dirtier and more bramble-torn it got. It actually made me feel more like an imposter. Like a girl wearing her grandmother's gown.

But cutoff shorts and a T-shirt were definitely not going to present the image I wanted, so I was back in the impractical gown. But I had added a new thing to my list of things to do when I ended my cabin vacation and headed back into town.

Someone in town must be skilled in clothing creation, I was sure. I knew my art skills would be a start, but I would need help making my drawn designs into actual garments that would fit on my body.

But it was past time for me to make the uniform of my office something of my own design.

And my own design would definitely involve pants. And tighter-fitting sleeves.

We reached the edge of the glade by midmorning, and I stuffed both of our travel mugs into my art bag lest we come into camp with too casual an air.

It didn't take long to find who we were looking for. The king was standing in the middle of the grassy field between the two camps, facing our way as if he were waiting for us.

And standing just behind his right shoulder was his daughter. Her gown for the day was a soft green that flattered her eyes, with golden thread woven both through it as well as through the braids that framed her face.

Something about her outfit was bothering me, though. Maybe it was all that gold? It felt a little too celebratory.

Not that I thought she was already dressed to celebrate the execution of Thoralv. Not even *she* was that cold and thoughtless.

But she was celebrating something. And given the events of the last few days, it definitely couldn't be a marriage of her own. So what was it?

I tried to look that question at Thorbjorn, but his attention was focused on the king long before we were close enough for the two of them to exchange words.

"Well met, Thorbjorn Valkisson," the king said with a nod of greeting.

"Well met, King Alarik," Thorbjorn said as we took the last few steps to stand before him and his daughter. Then he took my hand and wrapped it around his own arm, tucking it close at his side.

It was impossible to miss Lianna raising an eyebrow at this. She was far too deliberate with the gesture, and held it far too long. In fact, I had to fight the urge to grin at how unsubtle she was being.

But even her iciest glare melted before it could touch me. And then I had to fight not to grin at *that* little triumph.

"No, that is quite impossible," the king was saying, and I realized in my mute exchange with Lianna, I had missed Thorbjorn asking to speak to his brother.

"This entire matter could be cleared up in very short order if we could just hear what he has to say about what happened," Thorbjorn said, pressing as gently and politely as he could.

"I understand. But you know it is not up to me," Alarik said. Then he closed his eyes as if struggling to bring an old memory to the fore of his mind. When he spoke, his words were halting, but by his tone clearly final. "If there were a way around the promise he offered to my people and the haugealvs both, it would be perhaps not quite beyond the bounds of what I could do to give you a hint as to where that way could be found. But, alas, I find myself without the words to tell you what you seek to know."

It was kind of word salad, but I knew what he meant. The binding of the old magic included not being able to talk about the binding of the old magic. Much to his regret.

"I understand, of course, King Alarik," Thorbjorn said, and even offered a little bow. His hand resting on mine draped over his arm squeezed ever so slightly, and I added a little curtsy next to his bow.

Not that I thought I could perform that gesture properly. And to judge from the cold stare Lianna sent down her nose at me, I failed to nail it.

But I didn't care. It was just one more proof that her cold didn't have any power over me anymore.

The king had mumbled something else to Thorbjorn that I didn't catch, then swept away towards his tent in the skogealv camp.

Leaving Thorbjorn and me alone with his daughter.

"You look lovely today, Princess Lianna," I said. And I didn't even have to try very hard to make that sound sincere. She really *did* look lovely. It was suspicious, how lovely she looked, but that didn't change the basic fact of her appearance.

"It's an important day," she said. To me, but her eyes were on Thorbjorn.

"In what way?" Thorbjorn asked with a dark frown.

"What are you thinking, my little lord Valkisson?" she asked in an accusatory tone. "I am dressed finely because I am completely confident you will resolve all of this today. You will save your brother, which alone would be worthy of a celebration. But you will also clear the path for our two alv tribes to form our new alliance. And that is what I am dressed to celebrate."

"It would be easier to do that for you if we could speak to Thoralv," I said.

"I did offer," she said, but again with her eyes on Thorbjorn.

"How are you free to offer what your father cannot?" I asked.

Lianna just smirked. But Thorbjorn was not amused. "That is a valid question, princess."

"It doesn't matter. You already refused me," she said. From the hurt she put in those words, I knew she meant more than Thorbjorn refusing her offer of help. But he said nothing.

"We are looking for our men," I said. "I don't suppose they've been found in the area since we left here yesterday?"

"No. How could they? I don't think they were ever here," she said, deigning to shoot a glance my way, but only down the length of her nose again. She certainly enjoyed being taller than me.

Thorbjorn suddenly sucked in a breath, and I knew he had just thought of something important. But when I shot him a questioning look, he only squeezed my hand close to his side again. "Come, my love. There is somewhere else we have to be."

"Of course," I said. But I was suddenly so warm all over I was sure I must be glowing.

Lianna just sneered at both of us. "'My love?' I thought she was your volva, Valkisson," she said chidingly.

"She is. She's both," Thorbjorn said brightly. Then he steered me around until we were heading back the way we'd come, away from the glade and towards Villmark.

But Lianna wasn't done. She didn't follow us. Arranged as perfectly with the train of her gown spread out around her, the trail of her long red hair pouring over it, I doubted she could move in a hurry. Not if she wanted to preserve that perfect image.

Still, her voice carried after us without her even needing to raise it. Like she had magically amplified it, but not the way my grandmother sometimes did when she needed to be heard over rowdy crowds. No, this had a shiver of cold woven through its glamor and magic that was far from anything my grandmother ever employed.

"You've made a mistake," she said. I didn't look back at her, but I was pretty sure those words were meant for Thorbjorn. I looked up at him as we walked under the cover of the trees to see if her words had found their mark.

But he just smiled down at me as if I were silly to even wonder. "My only mistake was waiting so long," he said to me.

"No, that wasn't a mistake," I said. My own words took me by surprise, but at his questioning look, I slowly worked out what I meant. "It wasn't a mistake. I had to be sure of who I was and how I fit in here first. Here in Villmark. And I'm sorry that took so long. But if you had... well, if we had... you know. Sooner. If we had, I would've felt tied here to this place for all the wrong reasons. Am I making any sense?"

"Some," he said. "But as long as the wait has been, the road ahead of us is even longer. Yes?"

"Yes, I feel that too," I said.

Wherever Thorbjorn had been intending for us to go, it was going to have to wait just a little bit longer, as we lingered in a sun-dappled clearing far from the alv camps and Villmark both, and stole just a few moments together.

Because as long as the road of being together was ahead of us, that wait really had been too long.

And even now that we were together, I knew it wasn't going to be for enough time. Not nearly enough time. All too soon, this investigation would be over and Thorbjorn would be needed out in the wilds again.

But for now, he was close enough to touch. And that was exactly what I was going to do.

CHAPTER EIGHTEEN

When Thorbjorn finally got around to telling me what his thought had been, I was less enthusiastic than he had been expecting.

"It's just, when I talked to him before, he really didn't remember anything," I said even as we approached the last house on the top of the hill at the north end of Villmark. It was one of the largest houses in the town, but then again, it had to be.

It housed all five Valkissons as well as their parents, Valki and Gunna.

"It's been a day. Sometimes that magic fades," Thorbjorn said with certainty. "Not in a way where he can just answer my questions. But maybe if you try having him just describe things for you to draw again, there might be more hints in there. More things slipping through the forgetting spell."

"I'm only agreeing because I honestly don't know what else to try," I said.

I could go back to the crime scene and try drawing again. I could spend hours searching every inch of the woods around the skogealv camp in search of the missing Villmarker men.

But somehow, both of those things felt less useful than Thorbjorn's plan.

Which was saying something. I didn't have any faith this was going to be anything besides a waste of another precious hour of the last day.

Thorulv met us at the front door, almost as if he had been expecting us. He looked terrible, like he hadn't slept at all since I'd seen him last. Like he'd been drinking endless cups of coffee in the worst possible attempt at fighting his anxiety about his youngest brother.

"I don't remember anything more than yesterday," he said instead of hello after letting the two of us inside. Thorbjorn led me into a sort of sitting room that was on the north side of the house, far from the gorgeous views overlooking the village. The room was mostly in shadow, even though the curtains had been raised high.

But if I was going to try to get Thorulv to recall things from what his brain probably treated as a dream, this was maybe the ideal environment for it.

"Who's at the door, Thorulv?" I heard Gunna call from the direction of the kitchen. Then I turned to see her duck around the doorway of the sitting room. She and Thorulv were shoulder to shoulder—or rather her shoulder was at about his elbow, but still—and they both had the same curious look on their faces.

I looked down at my volva gown, but it was in no worse shape than the day before. And Thorbjorn was beside me, but not particularly close.

And yet the two of them were both looking at us as if they knew something had changed. Gunna covered her smile with her hand and ducked back out with a few mumbled words about fetching some coffee.

But Thorulv just glowered at Thorbjorn.

"We've just come from the glade and the two alv camps," I said, resisting the urge to step between the two brothers. Not that I thought they were going to fight or anything. But the accusation in Thorulv's eyes was going to hit Thorbjorn like a blow if he noticed it. And I was pretty sure he hadn't yet.

But he would.

"Did you?" Thorulv said in a low growl.

"I wanted to show you some drawings," I said. And my traitorous cheeks were flaming as I said those words. Which was crazy, because I had already taken that drawing of Thorbjorn out of my sketchbook. It was carefully laid away in one of my portfolios back at the cabin. No one but Thorbjorn and I would ever see that drawing.

"I'll just see if my mother needs anything," Thorbjorn said after an awkward clearing of his throat. He had to get past his brother to achieve this goal, and for a split second, I thought Thorulv was going to detain him.

But in the end, he just stepped aside, moving across the sitting room to the couch I was already perched on the edge of, digging through my art bag. I took out one travel mug and then another, but fumbled with setting them on the coffee table. Thorulv lunged forward just in time to catch them, which was lucky. They were mostly empty, but the carpet under that table was a snowy white. The smallest of dribbles would leave a stain I doubted I could magic away.

"I'm not angry with you," Thorulv said as he set the mugs firmly on the table.

"Oh?" I said, still flustered. And still not finding my sketchbook.

"We knew this was coming. The timing is..." But he just trailed off with a vague hand gesture and let the matter drop.

I finally had my sketchbook out and started with the drawings of the curved knife.

"We know this isn't your brother's blade," I said as I handed the book to him.

"No, this is the sort of knife the skogealv women favor," he said with a nod.

Which would've been handy to know the day before. It had taken hours to figure that out on our own.

The haugealv women had told us. But did that mean the skogealv men really didn't know about those blades hidden in their women's sleeves? But Thorulv did?

Some of those thoughts must've shown on my face, because Thorulv gave me a tremulous smile as he handed the book back to me.

"Out of all of us Valkissons, I have spent the most time among the alvs."

"Because you're the oldest?" I guessed.

"That, but once I formed that bond of trust with their tribes, it was easiest for me to speak for all of us when matters arose," he said. "I brought each of the others with me at least once, though."

"Thorbjorn made quite an impression on Princess Lianna, apparently," I said.

Thorulv frowned as if wracking his memory. "Did he? They both would've been much younger when they met before."

"Perhaps he made more of an impression this time, then," I said.

"I remember meeting her in years past, but not yesterday," Thorulv said. "I know she was the one who walked me out of camp, but it's like I know that I cut my chin jumping into a creek when I was three. It's not so much a memory as a memory of a memory. Or, like a memory of something someone else had told me."

"You've been under spells before," I said.

"Yes. I do not like it," he said. His hands were curling into fists, but his voice remained steady and calm.

"Let's start with that memory of a memory. Can you describe her to me?" I asked.

He didn't speak, just nodded mutely. Then he closed his eyes, still silent for several long minutes. I could hear Thorbjorn talking with his mother in the kitchen, their voices like a low background murmur. Someone else was with them. Not his father, but probably another brother.

Then that murmur became a kind of white noise, one I could sink my conscious mind into while my subconscious listened to Thorulv and drew and drew and drew.

When something fell in the kitchen with a loud metallic crash, both of us on that couch jumped and snapped suddenly to awareness of our surroundings.

"I feel like I fell asleep," Thorulv said, touching his own face as if to make sure it was still there. "Did I say anything useful at all? Or was I really just napping?"

"Let's see," I said, and turned back the pages I had drawn without really being aware of what I was doing.

I had started with a portrait of Lianna that I had rendered far more finely than she deserved. It almost annoyed me, how beautiful she was. Like my own pencil and art skills had betrayed me.

Then there were a few chaotic sketches of the near battle in the glade. I could recognize skogealvs and haugealvs, more as generic versions of each than specific individuals, but that made sense. I doubted Thorulv had known any of them by name, save the king and the council.

But after that—and turning the pages was like going further back in time—were a number of portraits of Thoralv. Thoralv with a mischievous grin on his beardless face, his spiky hair standing tall on his head. He even appeared to be spinning those blades in his hands like a stunt gunfighter showing off with his pistols.

But as I was examining each of these drawings, I heard Thorulv suck in a breath beside me.

"What is it?" I asked.

"Thoralv," he said, pointing at the latest drawing in my book. Obviously, it was Thoralv, but I just held my tongue and waited for him to finish his thought. "He wanted to go towards that glade. It was like he knew we had to be there."

"You didn't know the alvs were there?" I asked.

"*I* didn't," Thorulv said. "I don't know if he did or not. We were supposed to be looking for the men, but he wasn't looking around at all. He was heading straight towards the glade like a hound following a strong scent."

"He didn't tell you why?" I asked.

"No, he was being so mysterious," he said and rolled his eyes.

"But you turned up in that glade without ever finding the missing men. And you turned up right in the beginnings of a battle," I said.

"I don't remember a battle," he said, but waved a hand distractedly when I started to turn back to those sketches. "I guess a part of me remembers it, but *I* don't."

"Still, this grin on your brother, and his whole attitude," I said, going back to the last sketch. "He doesn't look like he knows you're on your way to break up a fight, does he?"

"No, I don't think that's what he was expecting to happen," Thorulv said. Then he closed his eyes again, trying to summon the memories back. "He was.... Well, you draw him with ease and happiness, and I guess that was there. But there was more than that. More of the other thing than of that blithe youthful ignorance you captured."

"Okay," I said, trying not to hear his words as a criticism of my technique. I didn't remember what he had actually described anymore than he did, after all.

"No, he had a reason for bringing us to that glade in the woods. A very earnest reason," Thorulv said, his eyes still closed. "He was very serious about it, which wasn't like him. That's why I followed him. I was annoyed at the secrecy, and more annoyed at the way he dodged all my questions. But that earnestness, that seriousness of intent, it was so very unlike him. That's what persuaded me. I had to see what had sparked that change in him."

"But nothing we've learned so far has given us any hint as to how he even knew the alvs were there," I said. "You two were patrolling together before you went looking for the Villmarker men. Was he different then?"

"No, I don't know when things changed," Thorulv said. "He's always had a merry heart, and no one ever asks what he has to be so jolly about. So that part was just normal. It was the sense of purpose he was radiating that felt new. I guess I hoped it was because of all the changes around here." He wove a hand around, and I understood he meant all of Villmark, not just the sitting room in his family home.

"The coming threat," I said. "The all too vague coming threat."

"Exactly," Thorulv said. Then he sighed. "I don't think there's any point in me trying to describe more for you, is there?"

"No," I agreed, putting my sketchbook away. "You remember the last few moments only dimly, when Lianna sent you away. And you remember the moments before you reached the glade fairly well. But everything in between is still only vague suggestions of things we kind of already know. You're absolutely sure you never saw this Tolkki fellow?"

"Not that day," Thorulv said. "He was dead before we even arrived."

Then he sat back with a surprised blink. "I didn't think I remembered that. But it's true. When we reached the glade, he was already dead and his body had been brought before the king. I never even saw the murder site. Thoralv either."

"This might not have been completely useless," I said with as much warm assurance in my tone as I could muster.

But as I went to find Thorbjorn, my heart was already sinking. The only thing I was more sure about now than I had been before we'd come to the Valkissons' house was that talking to Thoralv would clear so much up.

And yet that was something we definitely could not do. Not without agreeing to whatever bad deal Lianna had on offer. And maybe not even then. She had certainly made it sound like that option was off the table.

Time was running out. And I had never felt more helpless than I did in that moment.

But I mustered up something like a smile. Because the last thing I wanted to do was to let Thorbjorn see just how forlorn I was.

He needed to still think we had some hope. Even if I was starting to fear that we really didn't.

CHAPTER NINETEEN

THORBJORN and his mother weren't alone in the kitchen. There were two more Thors with them. Thormund, the second oldest after Thorulv, was pouring cream into an enormous travel mug of coffee. He had the longest hair of all the brothers, divided into three thick braids that fell past his shoulder blades. His beard was equally long, worked into two braids whose ends were tucked into the wide belt around his trim waist.

Thorge, the second youngest, was there as well.

Which meant he had been summoned away from his honeymoon.

And he had changed up his hair since the wedding. The sides were still shaved to show off the intricate knot work tattoos that curved around his ears, but the lengthier middle section that used to hang down past his neck was cut so short it was standing up on top, rather like a mohawk.

"Is Kara here too?" I asked him after I had given him a quick hug of hello.

He and Kara had been traveling together in the wagon that had once belonged to my grandmother's close friend Reginleif. Nilda, Kara and I had acquired it after Reginleif died, and had used it to bring all the Thors home after we had rescued them from the tower where some mysterious woman had imprisoned them.

Kara had taken a shine to the little home on wheels, and Thorge as a Valkisson was accustomed to moving constantly throughout the wilds, so Nilda, my grandmother and I had all agreed that they should keep it as a wedding gift.

"She's in town, but she went to see her sister and her parents," Thorge said.

"She and Nilda are going to help with the hunt," Thormund said.

"The hunt?" I asked.

"My brothers and the Mikkelsen sisters are going to search the woods for the missing men while you and I do what we can inside the glade," Thorbjorn told me.

"That's a good idea," I said.

"I called them back yesterday," Thorulv said as he fetched a travel mug of his own and filled it with coffee from the massive urn that stood in a place of honor at the end of the kitchen counter.

"So Frór is the only one patrolling?" I asked. The idea made me instantly nervous.

"No, Loke and your cat are out there as well," Thorge said. "Kara and I passed them on the road. They aren't going far out, but they're keeping an eye on things to the south."

"That explains that dream," I mumbled to myself.

"We should get back to the glade as quickly as we can," Thorbjorn said.

I nodded, but I really wasn't looking forward to another long walk in the July heat. At least this time I was prepared with my biggest sports bottle full of water in my art bag.

But the moment I thought of water, I realized I hadn't needed a sip of it when I had been at the glade earlier. The day was hotter than the one before, and I had felt sick the moment we had reached the glade the first time even though it had been at about the same time of day, after the same amount of walking and in the same not exactly appropriate clothes.

I wasn't sure what that meant. Was I just baseline better hydrated today, or more accustomed to the returned heat?

Or was it something else, something more of the magical side of things? Like how Lianna's cold glares were no longer freezing me?

"I'm sorry I wasn't more help to you," Thorulv said, interrupting my thoughts.

"You did all you could, considering what Lianna did to your mind," I assured him. "I just wish I could talk with your brother."

"They will never allow that," Thorulv said. "Not until the time comes for the sentence to be carried out. Perhaps then, as a final request, they will allow it."

"Hopefully it doesn't come to that," I said. I really didn't like the sound of those words. Final request. They sounded so… final.

We all left the house at the same time, Thormund taking up his mighty spear and Thorge his legionnaire's sword and axe from the weapon rack by the front door on the way out.

Yeah, the Valkissons have a weapon rack where most people just had hooks for coats. And with Thorbjorn not really having a preferred weapon but picking something different from a range of options each time he left Villmark to patrol, I was going to need to get almost as large of one for my house as well.

Just the thought had me blushing. Then I saw Thorge grinning at me as he tucked his axe through the loop on his belt, and I blushed even more furiously. He didn't say anything, but the wink he gave me said it all, really.

Everyone just knew the minute they saw me that my relationship with Thorbjorn had changed to a higher level. What was my tell? Did I look exactly like I felt, like I was floating six inches off the ground?

Thorge and Kara's wagon was waiting for us on the road outside the house's front gate. It was covered in spatters of dried mud, clearly not washed after its recent trip through points south, but the horses waiting to pull it were fresh, tossing their heads in their eagerness to go.

"We're going to ride there?" I asked as Thorbjorn opened the door in the back.

"Quicker than walking, although we'll leave it out of sight from the camps," he said. Then he helped me up the steps to the back of the wagon before climbing in after me and closing the door.

"Aren't the others coming?" I asked.

"They'll ride on top," he said with an attempt at a grin. But his heart wasn't in it, I could tell. "I thought we could get something to eat while we're traveling," he said. "Thorge said there is still some food left in here. As much as we can trust food from Alfhild, if we keep eating at the haugealv camp, the skogealvs will take offense."

"I could eat," I said.

We found the makings of smoked turkey and cheese sandwiches with grainy mustard and set to work elbow to elbow in the tiny kitchen space against one wall of the wagon. We reached past each other, or handed the knife back and forth, as if we'd made meals together all the time and had a comfortable rhythm all our own. Even in the cramped space and with the wagon wheels rolling in and out of ruts and rocking us back and forth nearly constantly, it still felt strangely familiar.

"I only really have one plan," I said as we sat down at the tiny table that was bolted to the floor of the wagon.

"What's that?" Thorbjorn asked as he sipped from a tankard of cool water.

"Drawing at the crime scene didn't show us anything, and neither did anything I drew when we were looking at the body," I said. "But I think there might have been sometime magical blocking me. All day yesterday I felt off. Like I had a dehydration headache."

"You should've said something to me," he said.

"I didn't want to the alvs around us to think I wanted them to bring me water or anything, because you said not to accept their hospitality," I said.

"Alfhild brought us water," he said. "Did you feel better after that?"

"It helped. But I didn't try drawing again after that. Not of the body or the scene of the crime, I mean. We just went home to the cabin, and I drew there. The only thing I can think to try is to draw again now."

"At the crime scene again?" he asked between bites of sandwich.

"No, or at least not at first. I want to sit down in the middle of the glade and feel all the energy of the entire place. Whatever happened, it ties into the negotiations, and the intentions of the skogealv king and the haugealv council both. Maybe I can pick up on some of that if I try drawing in the heart of the glade." I ended with a shrug, because it all felt so helpless.

But Thorbjorn was nodding as he chewed. He swallowed, then said, "I think that's a good idea."

"It's the only one I have," I admitted. I poked at the mostly uneaten sandwich in front of me. I didn't really have much of an appetite, but I knew I had to eat before we got to the glade. Magic could be draining, and I had no idea how much of it I was going to have to use.

But there was a question I just had to ask. "Thorulv said he summoned the others to search for the men," I said.

"Yes," Thorbjorn said, setting down the last bite of his own sandwich. Like he knew what I was going to say next.

"Not to rescue your brother? I mean, at the last minute, when all other hope is lost?" I asked.

"We are far from being out of hope," he said. Which didn't really answer my question. But after he added, "You've got this, Ingrid Torfudottir," it was really hard to press the point.

Thorbjorn's brothers halted the wagon well short of the glade itself. I climbed down, hoping to see the Mikkelsen sisters waiting for us, but they weren't there yet. And there wasn't time to wait. It was already past midday, and while the July days were still long, sunset was approaching far too quickly.

Thorbjorn and I walked together into the camp while his brothers spread out to search the woods. The day was even hotter than the one before, the air under the trees humid and close.

The feeling of being watched by unseen scouts was still there, growing stronger the closer we got to the camp.

But the headache and brain fog I had felt before were back. They hit me like I had run into a wall, then kept growing stronger. Even though I had been drinking water constantly on the ride over, so much so my belly was uncomfortably full despite the small amount of sandwich I had managed to eat.

I took my sports bottle out of my bag and took a long drink from it. The usually icy well water was still cool even after more than two hours in my bag, but it didn't seem to help. My eyes felt too big inside my skull, and my vision was distorted and blurry.

"What is it?" Thorbjorn asked me in a low whisper. As if he too felt the eyes watching us.

"It's back," I said, pressing a hand to my forehead. He caught my arm, forcing me to stop walking and turn and face him. He studied my face closely, even touching the back of his hand to my forehead. But I guessed nothing seemed amiss to him, to judge by the question still in his eyes.

"It gets stronger the closer we get to the camp?" he asked.

"Yeah," I said. I took another sip of water. It still didn't help. "It starts the same time that feeling of being watched starts."

"I wonder..." he said, but then stopped abruptly, biting down on his own lip.

What he was thinking would be dangerous to say out loud. But I was pretty sure I was thinking it too.

Whatever had clouded Thorulv's memories—whatever Lianna had done to cloud his memories—maybe she was trying it on me as well.

And, indeed, as I looked towards the skogealv camp in the glade, I saw her standing there next to a pale green tent. Watching us both.

I just looked up at Thorbjorn and nodded.

"What do you want to do?" he asked me, looking back over his shoulder as if to make sure the path back to the wagon was clear. In case I wanted to run away.

But that really wasn't an option.

"Press on," I said. Even as the light from the sunny glade ahead of us stabbed through my eyes and into my brain like needles.

I could see him fighting to find the words to say to me, both of us knowing that Lianna watching us meant she could hear us as well. Somehow. Acute alv hearing, maybe, if not outright magic.

"Is it worth trying?" he said in the end.

"Yes," I said, with all the firm conviction I could convey in that one word.

Because now that I knew what was going on, I realized why none of my other drawings in the glade had produced anything useful.

She was blocking me. She knew who I was and what I could do, and she was very subtly clouding my mind. Not as strongly as she had Thorulv, but enough to keep me from learning anything she didn't want me to know.

Not that I could prove it. Again.

But now that I knew it was happening, I could work around it. I could pull out my bronze wand now and dispel her glamor magic with a few choice slices in the magical world. I could end my headache and brain fog now with a wave of my hand.

The only thing holding me back was the idea of what could be gained in defeating her magic without letting her know that I had done so.

It would be tricky. I didn't know exactly how old she was, but I suspected it was older than she looked. And in any case, she had certainly been honing her craft far longer than I had even known about mine.

But if I could pull it off, it just might be the thing that saved Thoralv's life.

"The plan remains the same," I said to Thorbjorn. He nodded at once, and the two of us continued our carefully watched walk to the center of the glade.

But let her watch. I had found the way to defeat her iciness. I could find a way to defeat the rest of her magic, too.

Or so I really, really hoped.

CHAPTER TWENTY

THORBJORN and I made our way to the very center of the glade, where the indentations from where the stools for the skogealv king and the haugealv high council still remained, just barely visible. I chose a spot at the heart of that arrangement, set down my art bag, then fussed with my skirts until I could sit down on the grass without stepping on my own hem.

The end result wasn't as pretty as the king, with his many layers of garments laying just so all around him, but it would do. Dried grass wasn't poking into me anywhere, anyway.

I was just taking out my sketchbook and pencils when a shadow fell over me. It was tall, but not wide enough to be Thorbjorn or one of his brothers. I shaded my eyes and looked up to see King Alarik standing between me and the blue sky.

"I don't have answers for you yet," I told him.

"No. But this is how you get them," he said. There was just the slightest hint of a questioning inflection in that sentence.

"I hope to," I said.

"May I observe?" he asked.

But he clearly didn't mean *that* as a question, as two of his bodyguards brought a three-legged stool for him. I had sat so that I was facing east, towards Villmark, but they placed his stool just where the indentations remained in the grass, so he was still in the periphery of my vision just to the right.

"Ingrid?" Thorbjorn asked. He was standing behind me, far enough back so that he wasn't looming over me, but close enough to protect me if needed. I didn't have to look back at him to sense that he was resting his hand on the hilt of his sword. It was like I could just hear that gesture in his voice.

"It's all right," I said. "I can work with him here."

"We wish to observe as well," I heard Valeria say. Then she, Fedder and Rajka were there on my left. They had brought their own stools, but they too set them just where they had been the day before yesterday.

Before everything had gone so wrong.

"Of course," I said. This actually could help. They were all arranging themselves just as they had been. It would make my attempts to recreate the moment that much easier.

But then someone else came closer on my right. Lianna, taking her customary place at her father's right shoulder.

"Ingrid?" Thorbjorn asked again.

I closed my eyes and reached out with my senses. Just like earlier that day, I no longer felt the radiating cold coming out of her.

My headache and brain fog were still there. They hadn't diminished a bit since they'd reached their worst level just as we'd stepped out into the sunlight.

But they hadn't gotten stronger when she approached, either.

"Ingrid?" Thorbjorn said again. He was starting to sound concerned.

"I'm all right," I assured him. I tipped my head back, and he stepped forward just enough so that I could see him with the blue sky all around the sunlight glow of his red-gold hair. "I'm all right," I said again.

"If that changes, say the word," he said. Then he stepped back out of my field of view.

I looked back down at the sketchbook on my lap and the pencil in my hand. But I was suddenly sure this wasn't what I needed for the job at hand at all.

I put them both away, took a long drink from my water bottle, then took out my bronze wand.

I had never gotten particularly good at using it for magic, and what little I had done had always seemed to go better when Mjolner was there. But in that moment, it was calling to me.

I waved it around my head three times, almost like a baseball batter doing warmups.

Then I shifted it in my hand. I was no longer holding it like a magic wand. I was holding it like a pen.

And the air before me was my paper.

I had drawn in the air before, but only to invoke magic. I had never tried to make drawings in the air that other people could actually see.

But I had too large of an audience now for them all to crane their necks to look at the sketchbook in my lap. It wasn't just the king and princess and the high council. Skogealvs and haugealvs both were leaving the safety of their camps, inching their way closer to see what was happening.

But what they all really needed to see was what had gone wrong the last day of their negotiations.

Not that I knew what it was. Still.

But I knew a little. I could get a start. And if I felt out the crowd around me as my drawing unfolded, I might learn bit by bit what I needed to draw next.

So I started. I drew the king and the princess with the six skogealv grooms arranged around them as the sun was just beginning to set behind the tree-covered hills to the west.

And it wasn't so much like I was painting, but that the world around me was conforming to what I was creating.

The sun high overhead dimmed, and a second, redder sun began to glow behind me to the west. The glade was in ever-lengthening shadows now.

Nearly everyone around me had a ghostly version of themselves fluttering around them. The ghosts were clearly them, but in different clothes. The six skogealv men shifted until they were exactly in the positions they had been two nights before. Other people were moving as well.

But I didn't think I was compelling anyone to do anything. My magic, or at least my control of my magic, wasn't anywhere near that strong. It was more like this was a bit of live theater that everyone was very committed to participating in.

It would be interesting to see if anyone fought conforming. I wished there was a way to tell Thorbjorn to keep an eye out for anyone acting differently than their ghostly past selves, but I was too deep in the process of creating the illusionary world around us to spare the words.

I just had to trust he would come to the same conclusion as I did.

So the six skogealv grooms were flanking their king as guards, but also looking across the glade at the approach of their haugealv intendeds. And their live selves and ghostly selves both were smiling at the sight of the women as they stepped forward towards the center of the glade.

The six haugealv grooms were there too, flanking the high council on their stools. But their eyes scanned the skogealv tents in vain. There was no sign of the skogealv brides.

There was a long moment where no one moved. I could sense that two nights ago words had been exchanged, but my living painting didn't evoke any sounds.

Then the ghost versions of everyone started to move, darting about quickly. And it was like the living people didn't want to follow their past selves. They all stood rooted to the spot, as if unwilling to rush into violence so quickly a second time.

Which was probably a good thing, but wasn't exactly helping the case.

"We need to change location," I said as I let the illusion fall. The sudden shift in sunlight from darkening dusk to midday had all of us blinking.

I put a hand up in the air and Thorbjorn stepped forward to help me to my feet. Not that I really needed the help. I just wanted a moment to lean close and whisper in his ear, "Did you see anything?"

"The ghostly form of the young haugealv Alfhild was here at the edge of the glade, but her true form was not," he said.

There were lots of reasons why that could be true. She seemed to have more chores than the other haugealvs, or at least than the haugealv brides. It was possible she was just off cooking or serving food.

"What was her ghost doing?" I asked.

"Just watching," he said.

"Did she seem upset?"

He thought carefully before shaking his head.

I chewed at my lip. My gut was sure this was nothing. But my gut had been wrong before.

"Where are we going, volva?" King Alarik asked. It was hard to tell when the strongest flavors of his vocal tone were always cold aloofness, but I suspected he was genuinely curious under all that.

I put thoughts of Alfhild out of my mind and turned to the king with what I hoped was an air of confidence.

"To the south end of your camp," I said, pointing towards the evergreen trees.

"To where my daughter found Tolkki?" he asked.

It would be the easiest thing in the world to just say yes.

But when I opened my mouth, what came out was, "No. To where your daughter and the six skogealv brides are hiding the Villmarker men."

The sudden rush of sound around me was nothing like the sound a crowd of humans would make when something shocks them into furious whispers. It was more like the sound of a sudden breeze rippling the silks of their tents and pavilions.

But it really was the alvs whispering to each other. I could feel all their eyes on me.

"I will show you what I can, if you will just give me a chance," I said.

The king glowered at me darkly, but I steeled my spine and refused to be cowed.

I didn't look past him towards Lianna at all. I knew she was still there. Her zone of iciness was something I was always aware of, even if it was no longer touching me. But she said nothing.

"Very well," the king said at length. "I will see what you have to show me. But you should tread more carefully, young volva. You've already accused my daughter, and those words cannot be unspoken. If I catch you in a lie, there will be consequences."

"I understood that before I even spoke," I said.

Which was mostly true. Thorbjorn had explained it to me, and I had understood him. But I hadn't been thinking about it when I spoke. The words had just burst out of me.

Now I had no choice but to back them up.

I led the way across the camp, then sat down on the ground again just north of the tree line. The clump of evergreen trees where Tolkki's body had been found was just off to my right at the edge of my field of view.

Both camps remained standing this time, the haugealvs to my right and the skogealvs to my left. There was a definite no man's zone between the two that started just where Thorbjorn stood at my back.

I raised my wand again, and the world reverted to the reds and pinks of sunset. The trees before us were all in shadow.

But white forms were moving through those trees, flitting in and out of view like ghostly figures. That breezy whisper of voices rustled behind me at their appearance, but I ignored it, focusing everything on forming the image before all of us.

This was a moment in time that I hadn't seen, and that no one we'd interviewed had told us about. But the world around me held hints of it.

It was kind of like the trees themselves were aiding me. Not magical creatures who dwelled in the trees; all of those were north and west of where we were. No, it was just the trees. They had seen. And they remembered.

One of the ghostly forms drew nearer to the camp, her long white gown almost floating over the ground. Her head was bent forward so that we couldn't see her face, only the crown of her blonde head with its neat center parting.

Then she startled, like something had stirred within that clump of evergreen trees. She froze like a deer in a momentary debate of whether or not to flee.

A decision was made. She slipped her right hand into the left sleeve of her gown and pulled out a curved blade.

Then she moved towards the evergreens, her clothing and hair rippling off the ground all around her, like they were buoyed by wind we watchers didn't feel.

She paused again just outside the evergreens, and I was worried she would pass out of sight without answering any of our questions.

Aside from the main one. With that blonde hair, she definitely wasn't Lianna. I had no idea just how much trouble I'd be in if they decided I had falsely accusing her, but the twisting knot in my stomach was already sure it would be bad.

Then the figure raised her head and looked back over her shoulder before disappearing into the evergreens.

And I recognized her face at once. Well, to judge by the simultaneous inhalation of breath all around me, most of us did.

It was Lianna's cousin, the young Astri.

CHAPTER TWENTY-ONE

THE RUSTLING of whispers behind me became an uproar, and someone's hand on my upper arm yanked me to my feet faster than even Thorbjorn could react.

"That was not my daughter," King Alarik hissed in my face.

Then Thorbjorn was there, driving his body between the two of us and shoving the king forcefully away.

How fast had the king moved to get around Thorbjorn to me? I had been facing the other way the whole time, but I had seen enough vampire movies to have a good guess just how lightning fast that speed would have appeared.

That floating gown effect I had created in my illusion replaying the past hadn't been my own artistic imagination, then. The skogealvs really did move in supernatural ways.

"I never said your daughter killed Tolkki," I said, although I had to get on tiptoe to shout that over Thorbjorn's shoulder. "I only said she had helped Astri and the other five brides to hide our Villmarker men in these woods."

"You haven't proven that either," the king said. But he seemed to have his emotions back under control now. He waved back the guards, who had drawn their weapons and were awaiting only a sign from him to cut Thorbjorn to pieces. He had to turn and gesture to them again before they sheathed their blades.

Then he sat back down on his stool, the many layers of his clothing floating around him into their customary perfect arrangement without any aid from an outside source. Then he looked up at me with cold expectation.

"I didn't get to finish," I said.

"But we've seen who murdered your man," Thorbjorn said. "It was the woman Astri."

"Perhaps," the king said with deep skepticism.

"We've seen her go into the trees where his body was found with the murder weapon in her hand," Thorbjorn said, his voice a low growl that would have most men quaking in their boots.

But the king was not most men. "We saw only that much and no more."

"Surely that's enough to release my brother," Thorbjorn said, and took half a step towards the king.

Whatever he was thinking of doing next wasn't going to end well. Even if he intended to stop with threats and not go on to violence. The king wouldn't see the difference.

Indeed, the king was still sitting on his stool, as if completely untroubled by anything. But the look in his eyes as he watched Thorbjorn take that half step towards him was so clearly a dare.

He wanted things to end in a fight.

I didn't know why he wanted that. But I knew it was definitely *not* what I wanted.

"Please, allow me to finish," I said. I was speaking to the king, but I also put my hand on Thorbjorn's arm. I could feel the muscles there, tensed and ready to spring into action. But he seemed to remember where we were and what we were up to at my touch.

He took his hand away from the hilt of his sword and shifted his posture from fighting stance to patient waiting. Then he turned to me with an apology in his eyes.

"Someone needs to find the woman Astri," I said, looking from the king to the haugealv high council. "Before I go on with my spell, I need to see that she is here and will remain here until sunset."

"I will fetch her," Princess Lianna said.

Which was not what I wanted to happen at all.

"Not alone," Thorbjorn said, obviously of a mind with me.

"If you wish," the princess said with a very pleased smile. But that smile did nothing to bring the elements of her face into any sort of unified beauty. It kind of made her monstrous.

I hadn't seen her do it, but I totally believed she could move with vampire swiftness just like Astri and her father.

"I need you here," I said to Thorbjorn. I really hoped the squeak in my voice was something only I had noticed.

But Thorbjorn smiled down at me. "I know," he said.

Then he took the horn from his belt and blew a single blast.

That was all that was needed, just one short blow. The rich sound filled the glade, then the woods, then all the hills around us with its sonorous tone. I bet they could hear it in Villmark. It could maybe even be heard all the way past the magical barrier to Runde.

I heard the sound of breaking branches and rustling leaves behind me and turned to see Thorge and Kara emerging from the trees to the south. I longed to run and hug Kara hello, but we had to settle for a quick exchange of smiles. We both had jobs to do.

"Thorge, Kara, I need you to escort Princess Lianna in finding her wayward cousin," Thorbjorn said.

"We will go as well," Ilmar said, exchanging nods with Kallu.

There was a jostling among the haugealvs. Then Dres and Adla stepped forward. "We also," Adla said. Des just looked grim, but gave me the barest of nods at Adla's words.

I remembered he had been the one who had been matched with Astri. I couldn't even imagine what was running through his mind in that moment. Had he felt bonded with her at all? Or was this a relief?

But the current circumstances didn't bode well for anyone in the glade, really. If Astri were the killer, that still put the negotiations at risk. The skogealvs were still short a bride, even if the other five turned up.

None of my magical drawing so far had given any hint to where they had been two nights ago, or where they were now.

"Princess Lianna," I said just as she, with her six self-appointed guards, was about to head into the woods.

She turned back, her gaze as coldly aloof as ever as it travelled down her nose to me.

But then she stepped up so close to me that the only other person who could hear her words when she spoke them was Thorbjorn, standing beside us.

"I know you mistrust me, but I trust you," she said, her eyes mostly on me, but darting to Thorbjorn enough for us to know she meant she trusted both of us.

"You will bring your cousin here," Thorbjorn said.

"I will do as you ask. If what you showed us is true, my cousin has much to answer for," she said with as much sincerity as her cold tone could possibly hold.

"All the brides?" I ventured.

She bit her lip, just a single tooth barely pressing down on that perfect rosy surface.

"We need them here in sight," I said. I gestured to her green and gold gown. "You say you are dressed to celebrate. But there is nothing to celebrate without all six of them here."

That was the wrong tack to have taken, I realized at once. The blast of ice she directed at me may have blown past me without chilling me, but I knew she had sent it my way all the same.

"You accused me," she said, narrowing her eyes at me.

"You said you trusted me," I pointed out. "After I had accused you, you said that. What does that mean if it isn't you admitting to what you've done?"

She glared at me for almost a dozen of my anxious heartbeats.

But then she laughed, that merry laugh that sounded like bells. "I did," she said. Then she glanced over at Thorbjorn, who looked like he wanted to pull away from her, although she was making no move to touch him. But she just smiled at him with something almost like fondness. "I see why you like her," she said. "I wish the best to both of you."

Then she stepped close enough to touch her lips to his cheek. She didn't even need to get up on tiptoe to do it. She just leaned in a little to plant a kiss on him. Thorbjorn didn't step back or push her away. But the look he gave her when she finally pulled away was pure confusion.

"I know," she said with a sad smile. "My wishes won't help you. She sealed her own fate when she accused me in front of not only all of my tribe but all of our sister tribe as well. But I don't think I would feel the same about her if she had done any less."

Then she swept away into the woods, her six keepers falling in behind her. Leaving me fuming again at yet another conversation between the two of them where she acted like I wasn't standing *right there.*

"What will it take for you to release my brother?" Thorbjorn asked the moment they were gone from sight among the trees. He looked from King Alarik to the three haugealv council members.

"Your brother worded his own oath of parole," Fedder said. "He will be brought forth at sunset. And he will be executed if there is no other to put in his place."

"They will return with Astri well before the appointed hour," Valeria said, with the airy voice of someone speaking a prophecy.

Which didn't exactly fill me with confidence.

"He will be allowed to speak at that time, no matter who is there or what will happen next," Fedder said.

Which wasn't heartening either. It sounded too much like even speaking in his own defense wasn't going to make any difference.

But that couldn't have been the words Thoralv had chosen when he had put himself in their power.

"Astri will be here," Thorbjorn said close to my ear.

There was another crunching of boots over forest ground to the south, and for a fleeting moment I thought the seven were returning with Astri in tow.

But it was just Nilda, Thormund, and Thorulv. They must've been further away when they heard Thorbjorn's horn. Or perhaps occupied with other business.

"Any sign of the men?" Thorbjorn asked them.

"No," Thormund said. Thorulv's eyes were scanning the tents, the haugealvs and the skogealvs, and every other detail of the glade. Then he saw me watching him and gave a little shake of his head. Nothing was triggering any more memories in him.

"Perhaps if I go a little further south and a little further back in time, I can draw something of more use," I said.

As if I hadn't just shown everyone who the real killer was. That hadn't been useless, no matter what their stupid rules were.

"We will follow you," the king said with an expansive gesture.

I gripped my wand tightly, then stepped out of the glade and into the forest. I came to a small rise, not the one where the skogealv brides had confronted us the day before but a similar one. I sat down on the dry leaves of the forest floor and raised my wand.

And instantly felt my headache back. More than back, for the first time in my life, I understood what my mother had meant when she told me she had "thunderclap" headaches.

I dropped my head into my hands, desperate to get away from even the dim light of the sun that penetrated the canopy above. I heard a whimpering like from a wounded animal and took far too long to work out that I was the one making that noise.

"Ingrid?" Thorbjorn said in the softest of voices. He was squatting beside me with an arm hovering close to my shoulders but not quite touching me.

"Water," I said, not daring to lift my head.

He pressed my sports bottle into my hands, so quickly I knew he had picked up my art bag after I'd left it behind in the grass in the center of the glade.

Of course he did. He always quietly took care of me when I needed it.

And not just because it was his job.

I took a few sips, then tried a deeper swallow. But the headache was so intense I couldn't blink enough to make my eyes focus.

It was hard to think straight. Magic was definitely not going to be happening until I got this under control.

I had just raised my wand to try waving it around my head again when I heard a mocking laugh coming from somewhere in front of me and to the right.

There was a flurry of voices around me, but it was like I was trying to hear what was happening on shore while my head was underwater. Thorbjorn's voice was loudest because it was closest, but I still could no longer make out his words. Except I thought he might have said my name again.

There were more voices, male and female both, arguing all around me. And a scuffle, like someone was getting into a shoving match.

But the headache was not relenting. I wanted to lie down, but I was really afraid that changing my position would end in me vomiting all that water that was churning like acid in my stomach.

I pulled together the few working brain cells I had left. Not enough to make any kind of plan. Just enough to lift that wand one more time.

I couldn't dispel whatever was causing the headaches.

But I could point out the source.

I let go of all the usual controls I put on my magic that kept me from glowing like a delicious magic-filled snack luring in all the powerful beings that sometimes stalked these woods. I just stopped trying to contain my power, let it all go, and directed it towards something that was ahead of me, but also slightly to the right.

A lot of people had just come from that direction. Probably the seven plus Astri, or maybe even all six of the brides. I didn't know because I couldn't see. It took all I had just to keep that wand aloft.

But then I heard two women arguing, and then the crack of someone being struck by someone else's hand.

And just like that, my headache was gone. I could see. I could *think*. Whoever had been blocking me had been distracted enough by that blow to lose their own control over their power.

I lifted my head to see Princess Lianna standing before me, one hand closed in a fist.

And the white-gowned figure of her cousin Astri sprawled over the forest floor at her feet.

CHAPTER TWENTY-TWO

For several breaths, it was like the world around me was frozen in time. And it was such an amazing tableau that if I weren't so very much at the end of my rope, I would've loved to stay in that stopped world and just draw it.

I mean, Astri was sprawled with her golden hair and the long sleeves and train of her snowy gown spread around her in the most artful way imaginable. Her pale face was turned up towards sunlight that refused to penetrate the leafy canopy over her to touch her skin, although it dappled the ground all around her.

Thorge and Kara, the two skogealv grooms as well as the haugealv Adla were each clutching one of the other skogealv brides, as if they had to restrain the women also clad all in white from rushing to either Lianna or Astri's aid. It was a little hard to decide which, as the women in question seemed to have just in that instant started to slump in defeat.

Thorbjorn beside me had moved from squatting in concern at my side to lunging forward with one hand on his sheath and the other on his hilt, not quite pulling that sword out. He reminded me of a samurai, not just because of the low lunging pose, but because of the same unspoken threat that if he drew his blade, he could not put it away unbloodied.

Then Lianna moved, and it was like she broke the time freeze spell. All she did was release her fist and shake out her hand. But I could already see the damage her knuckles had taken. The pale skin over her knuckles was marred, and the soft flesh was swelling.

She looked straight at me without speaking, just shaking out her hand, as Thorbjorn let go of his sword and stood up, and the other skogealv brides stopped struggling to get free of their guards.

I honestly didn't know what Lianna was trying to ask me without saying it. But I found myself nodding, anyway.

"King Alarik," she said formally to her father, who was standing behind me and to my left. Then her eyes moved to the right, and she said, "High council of three. And all around me, from whatever tribe or people you are, hear me and bear witness. I accuse Astri of murder. We have already seen the proof of her actions. I demand the release of Thoralv Valkisson, so she may stand in his place."

"It will be done," I heard Fedder say. Then there was a rustle of people moving through a crowd to run back to the haugealv camp.

But my eyes never left Lianna.

I was annoyed that this was the thing I had been missing, the piece of knowledge that apparently even Thorbjorn hadn't known. Nothing we had done or could've done was ever going to free his brother. We had to get an alv on our side. And, just possibly, a high-ranking alv at that.

But I let that go for the moment. I had bigger fish to fry. "Where are our men?" I asked her. I narrowed my eyes at her. I knew I couldn't do the icy glare like she did. But I could remind her that I had still accused her of something she had yet to answer for.

"I will release them," Lianna said. Then she looked over at Bruna and Hella and gave them a nod.

Thorge and Kara were the ones still holding them restrained. They both looked to me for guidance.

"Let them go, but go with them," I said with a tired wave of my hand. "The men might need aid."

"They've all been well cared for, I promise you," Lianna said. "I'm sorry I didn't realize sooner what she was doing to you. But I've blocked her magic now. She can't hurt you anymore."

"Whose plan was this, daughter This kidnaping plot?" King Alarik asked. He had moved forward enough to be standing at my side, but seemed reluctant to close the rest of the distance to his daughter.

"Mine," she said with a bitter twist to her mouth. "Obviously."

"Why?" he asked. But his tone was more one of anguish than of anger.

Well, that, and betrayal.

"You do not agree that the humans are stronger allies than our alv kin?" she asked with badly feigned innocence.

"We have discussed this," he said.

"So have the haugealvs," I said.

I felt a twinge of regret for putting myself into the middle of their private conversation. But only a twinge.

I was starting to get the whole picture of what was going on.

Why Lianna had been chasing Thorbjorn so aggressively.

And why Lianna was wearing that dress.

"What do you mean?" Alarik snapped at me.

But it was Thorbjorn who answered him. "We know you are both fleeing from something stronger than either of you. Maybe stronger than both of you together. And you came here, to our very doorstep, to meet and discuss what to do. And yet neither of you thought to even let us know you were here."

"Whose decision was that?" I asked.

I was betting it had been Alarik's. And the furious flush of red that spread over his face said I was right.

"You weren't listening to me," Lianna said calmly. "I needed to do something drastic to get your attention."

"So you kidnaped our men?" Thorbjorn said.

"We borrowed them," Lianna said. There was almost something of laughter in her tone. But then she looked down at Astri, still unconscious at her feet. "I thought we all understood the gambit, but this one never seemed to get the point."

"What point?" I asked.

"That they were never going to be forced by me to marry the first six humans we lured into the woods," Lianna said. "She wanted to wait and pick one more to her taste."

"None of the six struck her fancy?" I asked. I was being a little bit sarcastic, but apparently that wasn't something alvs could recognize.

"We were never going to share them out that way. They were only taken to prove a point," Lianna said.

"What was this point?" the king asked.

"That the bonds we needed to strengthen were with the humans," Lianna said, with almost a hint of fire to her words. I would've thought her anger would've just been colder iciness, but apparently not.

"One of the men we grabbed was already married," Myrta told us in the smallest of voices. "We kept telling Astri over and over that we weren't actually going to marry these men, but she couldn't get it out of her head that Princess Lianna intended to match her up with a human man who already had a human wife."

"She took it as a very grave insult," Sibylle said.

"That's why she killed Tolkki," Myrta said, not quite looking at Lianna. "Because he was Lianna's intended."

"And none of you saw fit to tell me any of this," Lianna said. She fisted her swollen hand again, and the brides flinched. But Lianna's eyes were still fixed on Astri.

"You told us to keep to the woods and to hide with the human men," Sibylle said.

Lianna just sighed. But that was as probably as close as she would get to admitting the misunderstanding was at least partly her fault.

"My horn summoned my brothers, save the one you're holding," Thorbjorn said. "It also summoned our council. When they arrive, I will tell them all that has come to pass here in this glade. And then I expect you, King Alarik, and you, council of three, to meet with our high council. There is much for all of you to discuss. Together."

"Do you know what's out there?" I asked, shifting from where I was sitting on the ground so I could see the haugealv council as well as the king.

But they were all shaking their heads.

"Patrols have gone missing. Sometimes livestock and even children as well. But no one has seen who's responsible for any of it," Fedder said.

"But the auguries are menacing," Valeria said. "Vague, but disturbing."

"It's no longer safe to stay where we've lived since Torfa opened this place far from Old Norway," Rajka said. "Our barrows are too near the mountains."

"As are the ancient forests we've called home since that same distant point in time," Alarik said.

"There are safer places, closer to us," Thorbjorn said.

"I will give my suggestions to the Villmark council," Thorulv said.

"But we will negotiate promises of mutual aid and protection," Thorbjorn said. "If these skogealv women do not wish to marry to cement bonds, they will not be forced to."

"We didn't object to marriage," Myrta said, with a shy glance towards the haugealv Yanik. "We were only doing as our princess bid us."

"Without the knowledge of your king," Alarik said, and she shrunk into herself under the intensity of his stare.

I didn't hear anyone approaching, but I sensed the change in Thorbjorn's posture at once. It was like a weight had been lifted off of him. He was relieved. And then he was overjoyed.

I got to my feet, possible now that the headache was gone, and turned to see Thoralv and Thorulv embracing tightly. They broke apart with aggressive slaps on each other's shoulders, both of them touching the backs of their hands to their faces in ways that told me a few tears were being shed. But not enough for the others to tease them about it.

"Let's bring her to the center of the glade," King Alarik said, and two of his men went about lifting the limp form of Astri up off the ground. There was a general confusion of people moving about for a moment, but when it was done, most of the alvs had gone back to the center of the camp, including the king and the council of three.

Which left me alone with four of the Thors and Nilda. I took advantage of the momentary quiet to give Nilda a quick hug of hello.

"You do realize what almost happened here?" Thorbjorn was saying to Thoralv.

Who only laughed that merry laugh of his. "I knew you'd come, and that you'd sort everything."

"Did you even know what needed to be sorted?" Thorbjorn asked, gesturing at the stand of evergreen trees where Tolkki had been killed.

"Only in the larger sense," Thoralv said. Then his face finally grew serious. "They need our help. But they weren't willing to ask for it. Or, at least, the skogealv king was doing everything he could to prevent it. Not for nefarious reasons, though. It was just a matter of pride."

"And you knew all of this how?" I asked him.

He flushed at the question, but just shrugged. "I knew they were here. I came out this way a few weeks back, while it was my rotation home with our mother."

"Just taking a stroll?" Thorulv asked him skeptically.

"Exactly," Thoralv said. Then he laughed. "Best stroll of my life."

"Why is that?" Thorbjorn asked.

I felt a prickle on the back of my neck, that old being watched feeling, but not quite the same. This felt different than being tracked by a scout guarding a camp. It was more innocuous than that.

I turned to see Alfhild standing between the last two tents of the skogealv camp. She was lingering in the shade there, looking anxiously from face to face. But I don't think the others had seen her yet. They were all too intent on their youngest brother.

I slipped over to her. "Are you all right, Alfhild?" I asked her.

"I was working in the kitchen tent preparing dinner, but I heard something happened. Is it true? Is he free?" she asked, her hands twisting around each other in agitation.

"You mean Thoralv? Yes, he's not going to be executed after all," I said.

I was just about to ask if she knew him when I was forced instead to rush forward and catch her as her knees just gave out beneath her.

But she didn't quite faint. She caught my arms and clung to me gratefully, but soon was standing again on her own.

"Sorry! It's like I've been holding my breath for days, and now all the air at once is just too much. But thank goodness. I mean, thank *you*," she said to me with a grateful smile. "He said you would... I tried to believe him... Oh, just thank you!"

"Ah, there she is!" Thoralv said, interrupting what sounded like three of his brothers all chastising him at once. Then he rushed to push me aside and take little Alfhild into his arms. She squealed with delight as he spun her around and around, then fell into an understandable silence when he stopped spinning them both and just kissed her.

"I guess that answers that," Thorbjorn said, bemused.

"We still have work to do," Thormund said.

"Negotiations?" I said, trying to peer through the tents to see if the Villmarker council had arrived yet. But I couldn't get a clear line of sight.

But Thormund was shaking his head anyway. "No, patrol," he said.

My heart sank at the word. But Thorbjorn appeared at my side, squeezing my hand tightly in his.

"Not just yet," he promised me. Then he tipped his head toward the middle of the glade.

I nodded, suddenly hoping the negotiations drew out for days and days.

But in the end, with the arrival of the Villmarker council, they only took about an hour.

There were no weddings afterwards, but there *was* a party, and I got to dance the night away in Thorbjorn's arms.

And it was impossible to be sad when I was dancing in Thorbjorn's arms.

CHAPTER TWENTY-THREE

I WOKE in the morning to find Thorbjorn still there, and Mjolner newly returned.

Not that I could see my cat when I opened my eyes. But I could feel the warmth of his body against the back of my neck, the tickle of his fur in my hair, the thrumming rhythm of his purr.

"I thought you were going to sleep all day," someone said. Not Thorbjorn, who was still asleep. For one ridiculous moment, I thought it was Mjolner.

But then my brain woke up just a little bit more, and I recognized the voice and the sarcastic lilt both.

"Loke, why are you in my house?" I asked as I sat up.

"I had a remarkably similar question," he said with a smirk. "But you can tell me about it outside, if you don't want to wake him up."

"Please," I said.

He shrugged as if he had thought I might answer another way. Then he left the cabin, closing the door behind him as softly as he must've the first time.

I looked over at Mjolner, who was awake now, but was clearly waiting for me to leave so he could claim the entire pillow.

Thorbjorn was still breathing in the long, slow breaths that never quite turned into snores, but always seemed like they were about to.

I changed my clothes, then went outside. From Loke's words, I expected to find it noon or later. Thorbjorn and I *had* been up quite late the night before, celebrating with the alvs and with his brothers.

But the sun was just clearing the tops of the trees to the east. It couldn't be later than eight in the morning.

"How long have you been waiting for me to wake up, then?" I asked as I approached where he was sitting, poking at the cold remains of the last fire that had been had in the fire pit. I tried to remember just when that last fire had been.

The memory finally surfaced. It had been last October, when he and Thorbjorn had helped me clear Solvi's things out of the cabin after I had banished Solvi to the north.

The day that Loke had told me his full name. It felt like a lifetime ago.

"Not long," he said, still poking at the clayey remains of ash that had been covered with snow for months, then soaked when that snow had melted away.

"Did you only stop by to give me grief?" I asked as I sat down on the bench next to his. I stretch out my legs, grateful to be back in jean shorts and a tank top. The day was already stifling hot. Midday was probably going to find me seriously thinking about going down to Runde, if just for the refuge of one of the few buildings there that had air conditioning.

"If you wanted the two of you to be a secret, you probably shouldn't have told the whole town," he said with a grin.

"You might find this hard to believe, but we didn't actually tell anybody," I said.

"I don't find that hard to believe at all, actually," he said. "I know you. And Thorbjorn. And the town."

"Yeah. The town," I said. The Villmark rumor mill was running as efficiently as ever.

But then I took a longer look at Loke. Because while his words had been as teasing and sarcastic as ever, it hadn't sounded to my ears like he had really meant either. And *that* wasn't like him.

"It's about Esja," I guessed.

"Yeah, but not in the way you think," he said. Which was not something I was going to be able to parse after only a few hours' worth of sleep.

"Tell me," I said instead.

He didn't speak right away. It was as if the remains of the fire truly had his full attention. But then, still poking, he said, "You told me there were a lot of people in Villmark who would be happy to have her."

"There are," I said guardedly. "But why are you asking?"

"I'm not tossing her out, if that's what you think," he said with something almost like his old smirk. "No, I'm the one that has to go away. But I don't know when I'll be back. And she can't be alone."

"We'll look out for her. You never need to worry about that," I said. "That's a given. But now you need to tell me why you're going away."

"I need to," he repeated, as if he was trying to remember what those words meant when they fell together like that.

"You really do," I said.

"Mjolner knows," he said, still with most of his attention on poking the ash in the fire pit.

"You know he doesn't talk to me the way he talks to you," I said.

"Or," Loke said, sitting up a bit straighter, "you don't listen to him the way that I do."

"Either way," I said, not willing to take that bait. "I can't ask him and get an answer. So I'm asking you."

"I just have some things to sort out," he said with a careless shrug. "It could take a bit of time."

"Is Mjolner going with you?" I asked him. My throat was suddenly too tight, and the words came out kind of strangled. But I didn't know how to feel about either possible answer to that question.

I didn't want my cat to be so far away from me. I needed him. Especially when Thorbjorn left on patrol again. Which he was going to do, as soon as he woke up.

But, on the other hand, I really didn't want Loke to go out into the wilds alone. In fact, I hated that idea.

"No, Mjolner isn't going with me," Loke said softly, as if he knew all the feelings I was wrestling with and in a rare display of empathy had decided not to just tease me about them.

"I don't like the idea of you going alone," I said.

Loke glanced up at me as if weighing his answer. But then his eyes shifted to focus on something behind me, and that smirk was back on his face even before I heard Thorbjorn say, "He's not going alone."

My heart sank, and I knew even before I turned on that bench that I would see Thorbjorn there, fully dressed, packed, and ready to go.

And he was. And my heart found new depths to sink to.

"When was this decided?" I asked.

"Just now," Thorbjorn said as he crossed the yard to where Loke and I were sitting. "You need to go north?"

"Desperately," Loke said. But he had that wide grin on his face that made it really hard to know how sincerely he meant that word.

"Then I shall go with you," Thorbjorn said, as if it were already settled.

"I need to be alone," Loke said.

"In the end," Thorbjorn said. "In the north, you'll need to be alone. But there's a long road between here and there. And I shall travel that part of your journey with you."

"How long of a road?" I asked.

Thorbjorn just gave me a sad sort of smile and kissed me on the forehead.

Oh. So it was that long.

Loke's eyes darted from me to Thorbjorn, then back again. "I think I'd rather take your cat," he said. Again, his tone was in a Schrodinger's box, impossible to tell if he was serious or not.

"The cat is not offering," Thorbjorn said.

"Why are you? Offering, that is," Loke asked.

Thorbjorn didn't answer right away. He just stared at the fire pit as if he wished he too had a stick to poke the ashes with.

But then he sat up and looked at Loke again with a shrug. "Your sister needs you safe. Ingrid needs you safe. Villmark needs you safe. And I... I guess I just *prefer* you safe."

Loke licked his lips slowly, then even more slowly unfurled that wide grin again. "As much as I love the sentiment, I'm not sure that's within your power. But I'd love a little company on the road, for as long as that lasts. Shall we?"

"What, now?" I asked, my voice going all shrill. But Thorbjorn was already hoisting his heavy pack onto his back and checking the array of weapons on his belt.

And then Loke produced of all things a backpack that had been tucked out of sight under the bench he'd been sitting on.

That was when my panic turned real. It was rare enough to see Loke traveling in clothes that were appropriate for the weather. Loke packed for a journey was a sight that truly chilled my heart. It felt too much like he didn't think he'd ever be back.

"He has his own path to walk," Thorbjorn said to me, whispering close to my ear. Which I didn't think meant Loke couldn't hear him. Loke always seemed like he heard everything.

But I was too upset to care. Not that I could summon any words to form a response.

"I'm going to walk with him as long as I can. And we both have to trust in Mjolner. He remains the tie that binds us," Thorbjorn said in my ear.

"All three of us," Loke put in. Proving my mental point.

"All three of us," Thorbjorn said. I could feel his grin as his lips brushed my ear. But then he turned to Loke to say, "Give us a minute?"

"I'll head off without you," Loke warned as he walked towards the path that led from my cabin in the woods to the lands to the north.

"No, you won't," Thorbjorn said, still grinning.

"Why is this funny?" I demanded.

"It isn't," Thorbjorn said, studiously schooling his features back to seriousness. "It's just our lives. And I know Haraldr has told you the importance of shouldering our obligations while keeping a happy heart."

I wanted to cry at those words, but they were too true. And I knew they were true. So I just nodded wordlessly.

"You'll keep Esja safe," Thorbjorn said. "And I'll try to do the same for this rascal. But, Ingrid, I *will* have to leave him. I'll have to come home without him. I don't know what he's going to the north to find, but I know it can't involve me. Not in the end."

"I know," I said.

I had spent nine days alone, communing with my power. I guessed that Loke had to do something similar.

Only he had no mentors guiding his path. It was probably going to take so much longer than nine days. The whole process was going to be so much more demanding for him than for me.

And I kind of hated that I couldn't help him.

But I had to put those feelings aside. I just pulled Thorbjorn into a tight hug. "Just keep yourself safe, too."

"I think that goes without saying, my love," he said.

Then he kissed me good-bye. And if that kiss was anything to go by, it might be years before we saw each other again.

Not that I wanted to wait that long. But the heat from that kiss would last that long, for sure.

Then he broke away from me, resettled his pack on his shoulders, and brushed his lips against mine one last time before jogging to catch up with Loke.

Who, good to his word, hadn't bothered to wait at the edge of the clearing.

I rubbed at my cheeks, then turned to face my little cabin. My home. My place in the world.

And briefly I saw that cabin and that clearing both in all of their magical glory. Every spell I had woven into the wards anchored to the woodcut animals glowed brightly.

But brighter still was the glow from the home itself. Because there was now a second energy woven through those spells that hadn't been there before. It was nothing I had put in there, nothing I *could* put in there. It had a decidedly masculine feel.

But seeing it, I knew its light wouldn't fade, just like the warmth from that kiss was going to linger for months and months.

And looking at the spells that had woven themselves around Thorbjorn and me both as we slept, I knew he'd be back.

Because I wasn't just looking at *my* home anymore. I was looking at *our* home.

And that felt kind of perfect.

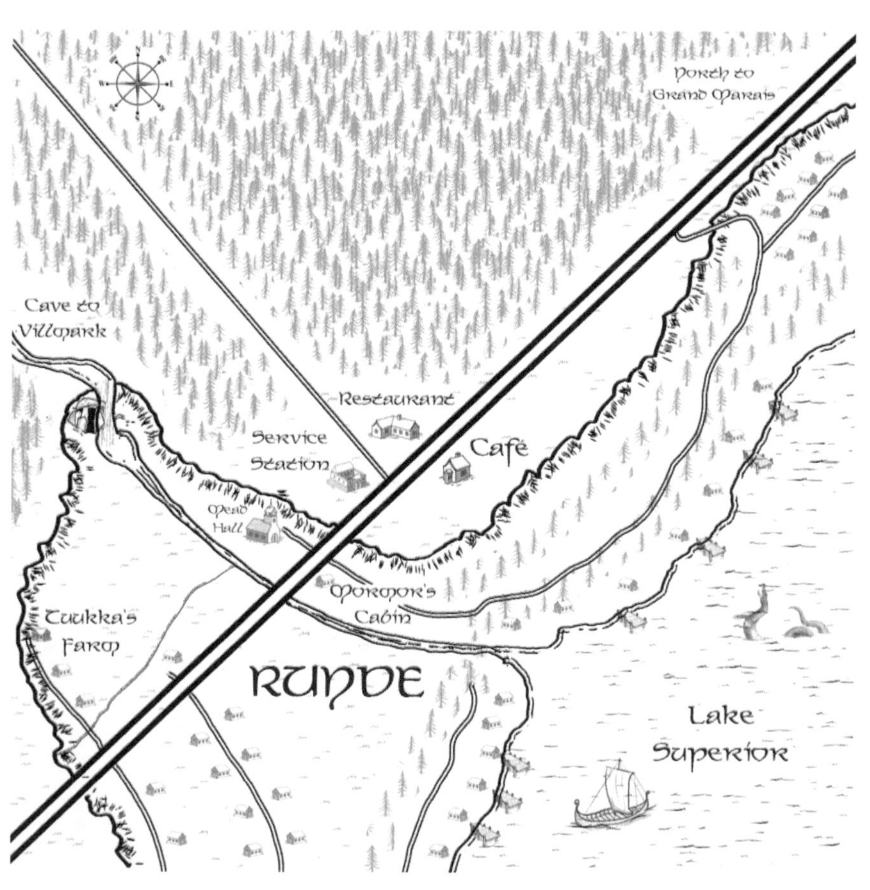
North to
Grand Marais
Cave to
Villmark
Restaurant
Service
Station
Café
Mead
Hall
Mormor's
Cabin
Tuukka's
Farm
RUNDE
Lake
Superior

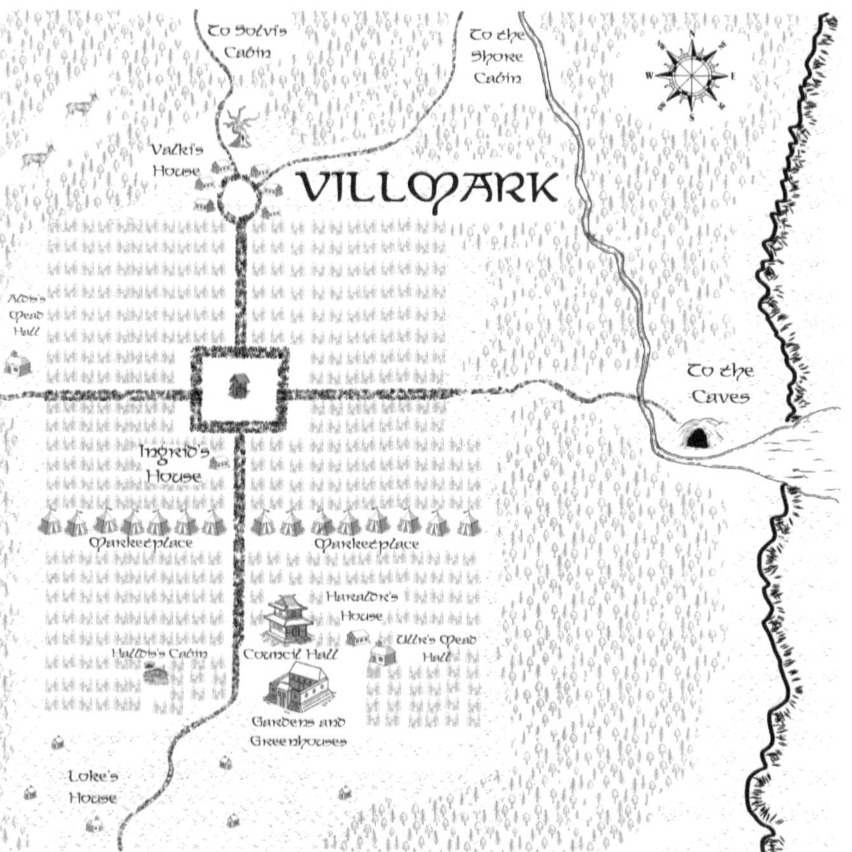
VILLMARK
To Solvi's Cabin
To the Shore Cabin
Valki's House
Aldis's Mead Hall
To the Caves
Ingrid's House
Marketplace
Marketplace
Haraldr's House
Halldis's Cabin
Council Hall
Ullr's Mead Hall
Gardens and Greenhouses
Loke's House
N
E
S
W

CHECK OUT BOOK TWELVE!

The Viking Witch will return in **Bewitchment After the Storm**, available now!

Ingrid Torfudottir juggled two separate lives for the longest time. In one life she struggled at aspiring to be a professional book illustrator, living with her grandmother in a Minnesotan fishing town on the North Shore of Lake Superior. In the other, she answered an ancestral calling to serve a village founded in the Viking age by Norse fishermen escaping some terrible enemy whose identity was lost to time.

Now she lives in the Norse village of Villmark full-time. Her house lies in the middle of town where anyone can find her. But loneliness is her companion now that her boyfriend Thorbjorn has gone far to the north to accompany her friend Loke on a mysterious quest.

But lonely doesn't mean bored, because life as a volva, a Norse witch, is never boring. And when a storm blows through, destroying all the crops and living too many signs of ill omen, Ingrid definitely has her hands full.

Then Loke's sister Esja starts to behave very strangely. Something is going on, and it's up to Ingrid to figure out what, before it's too late.

CHECK OUT BOOK TWELVE!

Bewitchment After the Storm, book 12 in **The Viking Witch Mystery Series.**

THE WITCHES THREE COZY MYSTERIES

In case you missed it, check out **Charm School**, the first book in the complete **Witches Three Cozy Mystery Series**!

Amanda Clarke thinks of herself as perfectly ordinary in every way. Just a small-town girl who serves breakfast all day in a little diner nestled next to the highway, nothing but dairy farms for miles around. She fits in there.

But then an old woman she never met dies, and Amanda was named in her will. Now Amanda packs a bag and heads to the big city, to Miss Zenobia Weekes' Charm School for Exceptional Young Ladies. And it's not in just any neighborhood. No, she finds herself on Summit Avenue in St. Paul, a street lined with gorgeous old houses, the former homes of lumber barons, railroad millionaires, even the writer F. Scott Fitzgerald. Why, Amanda can practically hear the jazz music still playing across the decades.

Scratch that. The music really, literally, still plays in the backyard of the charm school. Because the house stretches across time itself. Without a witch to protect this tear in the fabric of the world, anything can spill over. Like music.

Or like murder.

Charm School, the first book in the complete **Witches Three Cozy Mystery Series**!

THE WEAL & WOE BOOKSHOP WITCH MYSTERIES

In case you missed it, check out **The Teashop Terror**, the first book in the complete **Weal & Woe Bookshop Witch Mystery Series**!

No one knows more about every branch of magic than Tabitha Greene. She devoted years to studying the most esoteric texts, hunting down the most obscure source materials, and deciphering the most cryptic ancient scrolls. But her career in academia hits a dead end when no wizard will take her on as an apprentice.

Just because, despite being descended from two long and prestigious lines of witches, her attempts to actually perform any magic always fail. Often spectacularly.

But no more college means no more dorm life. And no magical skills means no real job skills, at least, not in the witchy world. And a life spent moving from school to school every few months was a life without real friendships. She finds herself alone with nowhere to go.

Then an uncle she barely remembers offers her a summer job, running his bookstore over the summer. The Weal and Woe Bookstore, located in a magical pocket world within a block of buildings just north of the old Mill District of Minneapolis, Minnesota.

Not exactly the pinnacle of all her hopes and dreams. But it's just for one summer, right?

Or so Tabitha tells herself. But unbeknownst to her, the Weal and Woe Bookstore is about to change her life.

The Teashop Terror, the first book in the complete **Weal & Woe Bookshop Witch Mystery Series**!

ALSO FROM RATATOSKR PRESS

The Ritchie and Fitz Sci-Fi Murder Mysteries starts with **Murder on the Intergalactic Railway**.

For Murdina Ritchie, acceptance at the Oymyakon Foreign Service Academy means one last chance at her dream of becoming a diplomat for the Union of Free Worlds. For Shackleton Fitz IV, it represents his last chance not to fail out of military service entirely.

Strange that fate should throw them together now, among the last group of students admitted after the start of the semester. They had once shared the strongest of friendships. But that all ended a long time ago.

But when an insufferable but politically important woman turns up murdered, the two agree to put their differences aside and work together to solve the case.

Because the murderer might strike again. But more importantly, solving a murder would just have to impress the dour colonel who clearly thinks neither of them belong at his academy.

Murder on the Intergalactic Railway, the first book in **The Ritchie**

and Fitz Sci-Fi Murder Mysteries, available everywhere books are sold.

FREE EBOOK!

Like exclusive, free content?

If you'd like to receive "A Collection of Witchy Prequels", a free collection of short story prequels to the Witches Three Cozy Mystery and Viking Witch Mystery series, as well as other free stories throughout the year, go to my website CateMartin.com to subscribe to my newsletter! This eBook is exclusively for newsletter subscribers and will never be sold in stores. Check it out!

ABOUT THE AUTHOR

Cate Martin has written stories which have appeared in **Mystery, Crime and Mayhem** quarterly magazine as well as in the annual **Holiday Spectacular** Advent calendar of Christmas stories. She is also the author of three witch mystery series: **The Witches Three Cozy Mysteries**, and **The Viking Witch Mysteries** and **The Weal and Woe Bookshop Witch Mysteries**. She currently lives in Minneapolis, Minnesota. You can learn more about her work at CateMartin.com.

ALSO BY CATE MARTIN

The Witches Three Cozy Mystery Series

Charm School

Work Like a Charm

Third Time is a Charm

Old World Charm

Charm his Pants Off

Charm Offensive

The Witches Three Cozy Mysteries Books 1-3

The Witches Three Cozy Mysteries Books 4-6

The Viking Witch Mystery Series

Body at the Crossroads

Death Under the Bridge

Murder on the Lake

Killing in the Village Commons

Bloodshed in the Forest

Corpse in the Mead Hall

Slaying on the Lake Shore

Bones by the Forest Road

Sacrifice Behind the Falls

Body Under the Café

Assassination in the Glade

Bewitchment After the Storm

Predator in the Lanes

Threat From the North

Snare in the Blind Alley

Ashes Beneath the Tree (available July 14, 2026 direct from me or August 11, 2026 in stores everywhere)

The Viking Witch Mysteries Books 1-3

The Viking Witch Mysteries Books 4-6

The Viking Witch Mysteries Books 7-9

The Weal & Woe Bookshop Witch Mystery Series

The Teashop Terror

The Salon & Spa Scandal

The Bookseller Blunder

The Entrepreneur Enigma

The Novelty Shop Nightmare

The Courtyard Conundrum

Short Story Collections

Bubbly, Bicycles and Brides

The Dorothy Lundegaard Mysteries

Fruitcake, Festivities and Firelight

www.ingramcontent.com/pod-product-compliance
Lightning Source LLC
Chambersburg PA
CBHW020502310726
48979CB00016B/2757/J

* 9 7 8 1 9 5 8 6 0 6 6 3 6 *